"Don't tell me yo
heat between us,"

Stacy held her breath, waiting for Patrick to lie.

"I've felt it," he said, his voice rough with emotion.

She leaned back to look up at him. She wanted to see his face, to read all the emotion there.

"I am attracted to you. But duty doesn't always allow me to do the things I want."

Heaven save her from logical, steadfast men. "You'll be right here with me. You said yourself we can't do anything else until the morning." She took his hand and kissed his palm. "I need you tonight. And I think you need me."

Patrick's eyes met hers, the intensity of his gaze pinning her back against the pillows and stealing her breath. "If you're sure this is what you want," he said. "Because once this starts between us, I don't know if I can stop...."

ROCKY MOUNTAIN RESCUE

—

CINDI MYERS

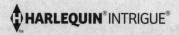

Recycling programs
for this product may
not exist in your area.

To Delores Fossen—my friend,
cheerleader and best roommate ever.

ISBN-13: 978-0-373-69749-6

ROCKY MOUNTAIN RESCUE

Copyright © 2014 by Cynthia Myers

Printed in U.S.A.

ABOUT THE AUTHOR

Cindi Myers is the author of more than fifty novels. When she's not crafting new romance plots, she enjoys skiing, gardening, cooking, crafting and daydreaming. A lover of small-town life, she lives with her husband and two spoiled dogs in the Colorado mountains.

Books by Cindi Myers

CAST OF CHARACTERS

Stacy Franklin Giardino—Forced to marry Sammy Giardino, son of notorious mobster Sam Giardino, Stacy feels trapped, until her husband's and father-in-law's deaths offer the opportunity for her to escape and start life over without the interference of controlling men.

Marshal Patrick Thompson—The U.S. marshal is determined to protect Stacy and see her safely enrolled in the Witness Security Program. He doesn't trust the mobster's widow, but he believes in doing his duty.

Carlo Giardino—Stacy's three-year-old son. He's the center of her world and she'll do anything to keep him safe, including partnering with a lawman she doesn't trust.

Abel Giardino—Sam's black-sheep brother is rumored to be Sam's chosen heir to take over the Giardino crime family.

Willa Giardino—Sam and Abel's mother lives with Abel on his horse ranch and is determined to further the family fortunes.

Special Agent Tim Sullivan—The FBI agent vows to close his case against the Giardino family, even if it means putting a little boy's life at risk.

Senator Greg Nordley—The U.S. senator from New York intends to be the next U.S. president and has no qualms about calling in favors to reach his goal.

Chapter One

When the first gunshots sounded, Stacy Giardino ran toward them. Not because she was eager to face gunfire, but because her three-year-old son, Carlo, had been playing in the front of the house, where the shots seemed to be coming from. "Carlo!" she screamed, and tore down the hallway toward the massive great room, where the boy liked to run his toy cars over the hills and valleys of the leather furniture and pretend he was racing in the mountains.

Men's voices shouted over one another between bursts of gunfire. One of the family's bodyguards ran past her, automatic weapon at the ready. Stacy barely registered his presence; she had to reach Carlo.

The living room of the luxurious Colorado vacation home was a wreck of overturned furniture. Stuffing poured from the cushions of one of the massive leather armchairs and a heavy crystal old-fashioned glass lay on its side in the middle of the rug, ice cubes scattered around it like glittering dice. But whatever had happened here, the combatants had moved on; the room was deserted, and the tattoo of automatic weapons fire sounded from deeper within the interior of the mansion.

"Carlo?" Stacy called, fighting panic. If any of those

stupid men had hurt her son, she would tear them apart
with her bare hands.

"Mama?"

The frightened little voice almost buckled her knees.
"Carlo? Where are you, honey?"

"Mama, I'm scared."

Stacy followed his voice to a dim corner under a
built-in desk. She knelt and peered into the kneehole
space—into the frightened brown eyes of her little boy.

She held out her arms and he came to her, his arms
encircling her neck and his face buried against her
shoulder. She patted his back and breathed in the little-
boy smells of baby shampoo and peanut butter. "Who
were those men, Mama?" he whispered. "They came
running in, and they had guns."

"I don't know who they were, darling. And it doesn't
matter." The attackers could have been law enforcement
agents, members of a rival crime family or different
factions of the Giardino family turned against one another. Stacy didn't care. They were all part of the cruel,
violent world of men that she had to navigate through
every day. That was what life was like when you married into the mob—always running and hiding, never
knowing who you could trust.

The family had come to Colorado on vacation, but
there was no getting away from the reality of their life,
from the danger. Her father-in-law, Sam Giardino, had
been at the top of the FBI's Ten Most Wanted list ever
since his escape from prison the year before. Which was
why they were staying here, on this remote mountain
estate outside of Telluride, instead of in a condo near
the resort like normal tourists.

And even while relaxing, Sam was directing the family "business," cutting deals, making threats and building up his evil empire. Putting everyone around him in more danger.

They could all do away with each other, for all she cared. The only other person who meant anything to her was Carlo.

She stood, straining to lift the boy, who was getting almost too big for her to carry. "I'm going to take you some place safe," she told him. "Just hang on to Mommy, okay?"

He nodded his agreement and she headed back down the hall, toward the stairs to the basement, where the safe room was located. The man who'd built this house—some billionaire who was a friend of Sam's, or who owed him a favor, since men like her father-in-law never had real friends—had built the concrete bunker and stocked it like those preppers she'd read about, people who were waiting for the end of the world.

Maybe this was the end of her world, she thought. Her husband, Sam's son, Sammy Giardino, had been battling his father for months now. Maybe those arguments had erupted into all-out war and Sammy was trying to wrest control of the family "business." She wouldn't bet against her father-in-law in that conflict; Sammy only thought he was tough. His father was the hardest, coldest man she'd ever known. He'd even pledged to kill his own daughter after she'd testified against him in federal court.

When she reached the top of the stairs, Carlo shifted against her. "They're not shooting anymore," he said.

Carlo was right; the gunfire had ceased. Muffled

voices came from the back of the house, but they sounded more like normal conversation than angry outbursts. Should she move toward them and try to find out what was going on?

She stroked her son's soft blond hair. "What did the men look like, Carlo? The ones with the guns?"

"They were really big, and they had helmets covering their faces."

Not any of the thugs Sam Giardino employed, then. She'd never known them to wear helmets. These men sounded like law enforcement, maybe a SWAT team. They'd found Sam's hiding place at last. Would they take Sammy away this time, too? She had no idea if federal agents could tie her husband to any of the Giardino family crimes. Women weren't supposed to concern themselves with the "business" side of things. In any case, Stacy never wanted to know.

She started down the stairs. She'd expected to meet others moving toward the safe room. Where was Sam's mistress, Veronica, and the cook, Angela, and the guards whose job it was to protect the women? Surely the cops wouldn't have gotten to them all.

But here she was, all alone with Carlo. Nothing new about that. Even in a room full of Giardinos she was the outsider, the one who wasn't one of them. They tolerated her and she tolerated them, but none of them would have been sorry to see the last of her.

How ironic to think she might be the one to survive this day. To escape. The thought made her heart beat faster. For four years, all she'd wanted was to get away from the hold the Giardinos had on her. She wanted to start over, somewhere safe with her son, where no one knew her and she knew no one. She didn't need other people in her life; she only needed Carlo.

As soon as the coast was clear—as soon as whoever had attacked the house had left—she'd find a car and drive as far away as she could. Maybe she'd even go overseas somewhere. She'd get a new identity, and a job. She'd rent an apartment, or maybe a little house. Carlo could go to school and they'd have a normal life. Just the two of them. Dreams like that had kept her sane all these years she'd been trapped. The idea that she might finally make them come true renewed her strength, and she all but ran toward the basement.

The basement was dark, but she didn't dare risk turning on the light. She groped along the wall, toward the hidden door at the back that led into the safe room. Inside, she'd be able to watch the other rooms in the house on closed-circuit television and see what was going on. The room had its own generator, its own ventilation, air-conditioning and heating system and enough food and water to sustain a whole family for a month. She and Carlo wouldn't need to leave until she was sure they would be safe.

She was halfway across the room, feeling her way around a stack of packing boxes, when she froze, heart climbing her throat at the sound of footsteps on the stairs. The tread was heavy—a big man—and he was moving slowly. Stealthily.

She cradled Carlo's face against her chest. "Shh," she whispered in his ear.

Light flooded the room. She pressed herself against the wall, hidden by the boxes, and blinked at the brightness. The scrape of a shoe against the concrete floor was as loud as a cannon shot to her attuned ears. She held her breath, and prayed Carlo would keep still. Her arms ached from carrying him, but she held on tighter still.

"Who's there?" The question came from a man, the voice deep and commanding. A voice she didn't recognize. "Come out and you won't get hurt."

She crouched lower and peered between a gap in the boxes at a man dressed in black fatigues and body armor. He carried an assault rifle at the ready, but had flipped up the visor on his helmet to scan the basement.

Carlo squirmed in her arms and whimpered. She patted his back. "Shh. Shh."

"Who's there?" the man demanded. He swung the gun toward her hiding place. The sight of the weapon aimed at her turned her blood to ice.

"Don't shoot!" she squeaked. Then with more assurance, "I have a child with me and I'm unarmed."

"Move out where I can see you. Slowly. And keep your hands where I can see them."

Holding Carlo firmly to her, she moved forward. The boy squirmed around to look, his little heart racing against her own.

The man kept his weapon trained on her as she moved out from behind the boxes. "Are you alone?"

"Yes."

He glanced around, as if expecting someone else to loom up behind her. Apparently satisfied she'd told the truth, he aimed the gun toward the floor. "Who are you?" he asked.

She met his gaze directly, letting him see she would not be bullied. "Who are you?"

"Marshal Patrick Thompson, U.S. Marshals Service," he said.

"Stacy Franklin," she said. Franklin was her maiden name, but she didn't have any desire to introduce herself to this lawman as one of the Giardinos. "And this is my son, Carlo."

"Hello, Carlo." He nodded to the boy. His expression was still wary, but he had kind eyes, blue, with lines fanning out from the corners, as if he'd spent a lot of time outdoors, squinting into the sun. Carlo stared at him, wide-eyed, his fingers in his mouth.

Thompson turned his attention back to Stacy. "I'll need you to come with me," he said.

"Come with you where?"

"First, upstairs. We'll take a preliminary statement from you, and then I'll need you to come with me to our headquarters in Telluride."

"Are you arresting me? I haven't done anything wrong."

"No, I'm not arresting you, but you are a witness, and we may need to take you into protective custody."

She had no intention of letting anyone take her into custody, but she kept that to herself. She knew the law; though Sammy had been the one with the law degree, Stacy had written all his papers and helped him study for all his tests. She'd read the textbooks and listened to the online lectures and studied alongside him for the bar exam. None of it was knowledge the Giardinos thought a woman needed to know, but she would use it to her advantage now.

"Why are you here?" she asked.

Marshal Thompson didn't answer. He motioned for

her to move ahead of him. "Come with me upstairs and we'll talk more."

She climbed the stairs, aware of him right behind her, a broad-shouldered, black-clad guardian who smelled strongly of cordite and hot steel from his weapon, which must have recently been fired.

He led her into the living room, where other men milled about, taking pictures and measurements. She sat. Carlo scrambled out of her arms and retrieved one of his toy cars and began driving it along the arm of the sofa.

Marshal Thompson removed his helmet and sat on the arm of the sofa, his weapon on the table beside him. He had short, light brown hair and he looked tired—as tired as Stacy suddenly felt. "What is your relationship to the Giardino family?" he asked.

She thought about lying, saying she was a maid. But they'd check her story and learn her real identity soon enough. She lifted her chin, defiant. "I'm married to Sammy Giardino."

His gaze shifted to Carlo, who was making motor noises, guiding the toy car along a seam in the leather upholstery. "This is Sammy's son?"

"Yes." She patted his chubby leg in the corduroy overalls he was already outgrowing. He was *her* son— Sammy had contributed half his DNA, but she had given the boy her heart and soul. He was the one thing that had kept her sane in this crazy household.

"How long have you been in this house?"

She should probably demand a lawyer, or refuse to answer his questions altogether. But she didn't really care about the answers. The sooner she told him what he wanted to know, the sooner he'd let her go. "We arrived on Sunday. Five days ago." Five days of unrelenting tension in which Sammy alternately sulked and sniped, while his father looked smug. Visitors came and went at all hours, and twice she'd awakened deep in the night to hear arguments between father and son, shouting matches she'd fully expected to end in a hail of bullets.

"Why did you come to Telluride?" Thompson asked.

Because I didn't have the option of staying behind, she thought. "We came on vacation," she said. "To ski." Carlo had loved the snow. He'd spent two half days in kiddie ski school, thrilled by the rare opportunity to hang out with boys and girls his own age. It was tough to arrange playdates when you lived with a mobster.

"Who else is in the house?"

"A lot of people. I don't even know all their names." This wasn't exactly true, but she was wary of telling Thompson anything he didn't already know, like the fact that her fugitive father-in-law had been here. If Sam had managed to escape, she didn't want him finding out she was the one who had betrayed him.

"Any other women?" Thompson asked.

Why did Thompson care about the women? "There was the cook, Angie. A woman named Veronica." No point explaining her role as Sam's latest mistress. "My sister-in-law, Elizabeth Giardino." Elizabeth had been a big surprise, showing up for lunch today as if her father had never threatened to murder her.

"That's all?"

She looked up at him through the fringe of her lashes. "All the women."

"And the men?"

She looked around the room, at the masculine furniture and big-screen television, at the black-clad men who dusted for fingerprints and took photographs from every angle. "There were a lot of men here. There always are." The women were merely ornaments. Accessories. Necessary for carrying on the family name, but otherwise in the way. They were kept in the background as much as possible.

"Was there anyone here who wasn't a member of the family?"

"You mean besides all the bodyguards?"

"Besides them, yes. Any visitors?"

"Elizabeth was a visitor. She doesn't live here."

"Anyone else?"

She shook her head. "But I don't keep track of everyone who comes and goes."

"Because you're not interested?"

"That, and because I don't want to know about the Giardino business."

"Sir, the M.E. says he's finished in the library," one of the black-clad officers addressed Thompson.

Thompson nodded. "All right. Then you can seal off the room."

"Where is everyone?" Stacy asked. The first shock of the invasion had worn off and uneasiness stole over her like a virus, making her feel sick and a little dizzy. "The other women and the rest of the family."

"They're being taken care of. You were the only one unaccounted for. Where were you when the shooting started?"

"In the bathroom, if that really makes any difference."

The double doors leading into the hall opened and

a man in black backed into the room, wheeling a gurney. Stacy stared at the figure on the gurney, covered by a white sheet. A bone-deep chill swept through her. "Who is that?" she asked, forcing the words out.

"Mrs. Giardino—" Thompson put out his arm to stop her, but she threw off his grasp and ran to the gurney.

The men wheeling it past stopped and looked at Thompson. "Sir?"

"It's all right." Thompson glanced at Carlo, who had crawled under the coffee table and was absorbed in orchestrating elaborate car crashes. "Let her look."

She hesitated, staring at the outline of a face under the white sheet, afraid of what she'd see there, yet knowing she had to look.

The man at the head of the gurney leaned over and flipped back the sheet.

Stacy gasped and covered her mouth with her hand. Thompson's hand rested heavy on her shoulder. "Can you identify this man for me, please?" he asked.

"That's my husband," she whispered. In death, he looked older than she remembered, his skin waxy and slack, the cruelty gone from his expression. "That's Sammy," she breathed, and staggered back into the marshal's arms.

Chapter Two

Marshal Patrick Thompson considered himself a good judge of character, but he wasn't sure what to make of Stacy Franklin Giardino. When he'd stepped into the basement of that backcountry mansion, the last person he'd expected to encounter was this woman who looked like a college girl or a rock star, not a mobster's wife. She was all of five foot two and probably weighed ninety pounds soaking wet. She had fine, sharp features and huge gray eyes, and her short, platinum blond hair only made her look more elfin and vulnerable.

Dressed in leggings, an oversize sweater and short leather boots, she looked more like the little boy's big sister or babysitter than his mother, but a double-check of the background files on the Giardino family confirmed she was indeed the wife—or make that, the widow—of the late Sam Giardino Junior, and the boy, Carlo, was the heir apparent of the Giardino mob family.

Patrick stood in a darkened office at the police station the feds were using as their temporary base in Telluride and studied Stacy and her son through a one-way mirror. The boy was eating cookies, painstakingly separating each cookie into two halves, licking all the filling out and then nibbling away the cookie portions. Stacy watched her son, scarcely moving except to occasionally cross and uncross her legs.

Nice legs, he thought, though he told himself he wasn't supposed to notice them. He wasn't supposed to think of the women he was assigned to protect that way. They were victims or suspects or witnesses. But he was a healthy, single man and sometimes…

"What do you think?"

Patrick flinched, and looked over his shoulder at the man who spoke, FBI special agent Tim Sullivan. Though his first impulse was to say that Stacy was a very appealing woman, he knew that wasn't what Sullivan wanted to know. "She says she doesn't know anything about the Giardinos' crimes—that the women were kept in the dark."

"Do you think she's telling the truth?"

"Maybe." Patrick turned to look at Stacy again. Beneath the carefully applied makeup he detected dark circles of fatigue beneath her eyes. Earlier, she'd been so fierce, like a mother bear protecting her cub. Now she looked more vulnerable. "What makes a woman align herself with a criminal like Sammy Giardino?" he asked.

Sullivan moved to stand beside him. "Maybe she didn't know he was a crook until it was too late."

"Then why not leave? Why stay in a marriage with a man like that?"

"That answer's easy. You don't divorce a mobster. You know enough about them to be dangerous, and as long as you're married, you can't be compelled to testify against them."

Had Stacy been trapped like that? The thought made

his stomach twist. "She had to have known what he was like before they married," he said. "The background report on her says her father is a shipping merchant who's suspected of having some shady dealings with the Giardino family."

As if sensing someone watching, she turned and looked directly into the mirror. Her eyes were hard and cold. So much for thinking she was vulnerable. He'd seen women like her before. They were hostile to law enforcement, uncooperative and difficult. But it was his job to protect her, so he would.

"You want me to talk to her?" Sullivan asked.

"No, I'll do it." Patrick picked up a file folder from the corner of the desk and stepped out into the hall.

Stacy looked up when he entered the room. Carlo had finished his cookies and lay stretched across two chairs, his head in his mother's lap. "When can we go?" she asked, her voice just above a whisper. "It's going to be Carlo's bedtime soon."

"I'll drive you to your hotel soon." He sat, one hip on the table beside her, a casual pose that was supposed to help her relax, but there was nothing at ease about the rigid set of her shoulders. With one hand she smoothed her son's hair, over and over. "We'll provide protection for you until we're sure you and your son are safe. If we decide to press charges against anyone else, you may be asked to testify, and in that case you'll be under our protection until the trial. After that, you'll have the option of going into Witness Security and assuming a new identity."

"No." The hand that had been stroking her son stilled. "I won't do that."

Not an unusual reaction to the idea of starting life over as someone else. It took time for most people to come around. "You and your son could be in danger," he said.

"I can take care of my son."

"We can talk about this more later. For now, you'll be assigned an agent for protection."

If looks really could kill, the hate-filled stare she directed at him would have felled him like a shot. He pretended not to notice. "Do you have family you want us to notify—parents, siblings?" he asked.

"I'm an only child."

"Your parents, then." He consulted the notes in the file. "Your mother and father, Debby and George Franklin, live in Queens?"

"I don't want to see them."

"Why not?" Had there been a rift when she married Giardino?

"That's none of your business."

He conceded the point and let his gaze drift to the boy. The key with a hostile witness was to find some point of connection. "How is your son?"

"He's tired and confused. He wants to go home." Her expression softened and she stroked the boy's hair again—a honey color several shades darker than her own. "I haven't told him about his father yet. I'm not sure he'd understand."

"And how are you doing?"

The hardness returned. "If you're worried I'm all torn up because my husband's dead, don't be."

"So you're not upset?"

"I'm not. I hated him."

"Then why did you marry him?"

She shook her head. "You wouldn't understand."

"Try me."

She pressed her lips together in a thin line. He thought she wasn't going to say anything, but he waited anyway. Had she really hated her husband, or was this a ploy to distance herself further from the Giardinos and their crimes? "My father and his father arranged for us to get married," she said. "I scarcely even knew him."

"Come on. This is the twenty-first century. And it's America, not the old country."

Her expression clouded. "I told you you wouldn't understand."

He let the words hang between them, hoping she'd elaborate, but she did not. She didn't look away from him either, but kept her gaze steady and challenging, unflinching.

He shifted, and his leg brushed against her arm. She flinched and he moved away. This wasn't right, him looming over her this way. He pulled up a chair and sat beside her, turned to face her. "I wanted to ask you a few more questions about today," he said.

"I can't tell you anything about the Giardinos."

"You were married to Sam Giardino's son for four years. You lived in the Giardino family home during all that time. I believe you know more than you think you know. Did people often come to the house to discuss business?"

She remained silent.

He removed a photograph from the folder—an eight-by-ten glossy used by Senator Greg Nordley in his campaign. "Have you seen this man before? At the house or with Sam or Sammy somewhere else?"

She scarcely glanced at the photo. "Where are the other women—Victoria and Elizabeth? Have you asked them these questions?"

The women were at this moment in other interrogation rooms, being questioned by other officers. "They're safe. And yes, we're talking to them."

"They'll tell you the same thing I will—we don't know anything. We weren't allowed to know anything. Women in the Giardino household were like furniture or children—to be seen and not heard."

"I'm surprised you put up with that kind of treatment."

Anger flared, putting color in her cheeks and life in her eyes. She looked more striking than ever. "You think I had a choice?"

"You strike me as an outspoken, independent young woman. Not someone who'd let herself be bullied." When she'd stepped out into the basement, the boy in her arms, she'd looked ready to take him on, despite the fact that she was unarmed.

She looked away, but not before he caught a glimpse of sadness—or was it despair?—in her eyes. "If you lived in a household with men who thought nothing of cutting a man's face off if he said something they didn't like, would you be so eager to speak up?"

"Are you saying the Giardinos threatened you?"

"They didn't think of them as threats. Call them promises."

"Did they physically abuse you?" His anger was a

sharp, heavy blade at the back of his throat, surprising in its intensity.

She shook her head. "It doesn't matter."

He shifted, wanting to put some distance between himself and this woman who unsettled him so. She was alternately cold and vulnerable, in turns innocent and calculating. He pretended to consult the file folder, though the words blurred before an image of Stacy, cowering before a faceless thug with a gun.

"Does the name Senator Nordley mean anything to you?" he asked, forcing the disturbing image away.

"He's a senator from New York. What is this, a civics test?"

"We believe the senator was at the house shortly before we broke in this afternoon."

"I didn't see him."

"Did you see Sam Giardino with anyone in the past few days who was not a regular part of the household?"

"No. I stayed as far away from Sam as I could."

"Why is that?"

"He and my husband were fighting. I didn't want to get caught in the cross fire. Literally."

"What were they fighting about?"

"Control of the family. Sammy wanted his father to give him more say in day-to-day operations, but Sam refused."

"But Sam was the natural successor to his father, wasn't he?"

"Supposedly. But Sam used to taunt him. He'd threaten to pass over Sam and hand the reins over to his brother, Sammy's Uncle Abel."

Patrick leafed through the folder. He found no mention of anyone named Abel. "Who was Uncle Abel?"

"Sam's younger brother. He was the black sheep no one ever talked about—because he wouldn't go into the family business."

"But Sam threatened to turn things over to him instead of to Sammy?"

"It was just his way of getting back at Sammy. Abel had nothing to do with the business and hadn't for years."

"Where is Abel now?"

"He and Sam's mother—Sammy's grandmother—live on a ranch somewhere in Colorado."

The hairs on the back of Patrick's neck stood up. There was something to this Abel Giardino. Maybe the Colorado connection they'd been looking for. "Did you ever meet Abel?"

"He and the grandmother came to our wedding. He looked like some old cowboy."

"And the mother?"

"The mother was scarier than either of her sons. She didn't approve of me and threatened to give me the evil eye if I wasn't good to her only grandson." Stacy shuddered, and rubbed her hands up and down her arms. "After meeting her, I know why Sam was so mean."

"All the more reason for us to offer you protection."

"I told you, I don't want your protection!"

At the sound of her raised voice, Carlo stirred and whimpered. She bent over him and made soothing noises. In that instance she transformed from cold and angry to warm and tender. The contrast struck him, made him feel sympathy for her, though he didn't want to. She was a member of a crime family, probably a criminal herself. She didn't deserve his sympathy.

When the boy had settled back to sleep, she looked at Patrick again. "Please, just let us leave," she said.

He stood. "I'll have someone take you to your hotel."

He left the room, shutting the door softly behind him. He found Sullivan in his office down the hall. "Have you heard of Abel Giardino?" Patrick asked.

Sullivan shook his head. "Who is he?"

"Sam's brother. He supposedly was never involved in the family's crimes. He lives with his mother somewhere in Colorado."

"Could he be the reason Sam was in the state?"

"It would be worth checking out. Stacy says Sam talked about choosing his brother to succeed him as head of the family, instead of Sam Junior."

Sullivan made a note. "Did you get anything else out of her?"

"Only that she apparently hated her husband's guts. And she doesn't appear to have fond feelings for any of the rest of the family."

"No confirmation on the senator?"

"She said she hadn't seen him around."

"Do you think she's telling the truth?"

"Hard to say. She's not one to give anything away. I'll ask Sergeant Robinson to take her and the boy to the hotel for the night and we'll try again in the morning."

He called the sergeant's extension and gave the officer his orders: take Mrs. Giardino and her son to the hotel they'd selected and stay on guard until someone else came to relieve him.

He returned to his office and sat back in his desk

chair. He liked to review a witness's answers while they were fresh in his mind. He looked for patterns and inconsistencies, for vulnerabilities he could exploit or new information he needed to explore further. Certainly, he wanted to know more about Abel. But he wanted to know more about Stacy, too, and how she fit into this sordid picture of a family of criminals.

Instead of thinking about what Stacy had said, his thoughts turned to everything she hadn't said. Why had her father and Sam arranged for her to marry Sammy— if that had indeed happened? What had the Giardinos done to make her so afraid? Was she really as ignorant of their dealings as she claimed?

And why did she get to him, making him forget himself and want to comfort her? Protect her? Was she just a good actress, accomplished at manipulating men, or was something else going on here? He needed to understand so he could avoid making a wrong move in the future.

A sharp knock sounded on the door. "Come in."

Sergeant Robinson, a thin, balding officer, leaned in. "Sir?"

"What is it, Sergeant? Why aren't you with Mrs. Giardino?"

The sergeant's gaze darted around the office, as if he expected to find Stacy Giardino standing in the corner. "She's not with you?"

"No. She's in interview room two. I told you that."

The sergeant swallowed, his Adam's apple bobbing. "The interview room is empty, sir. Mrs. Giardino is gone."

Chapter Three

Stacy wasn't about to wait around for Sergeant What's-his-name to haul her off to a hotel room that would be little better than a prison. She'd had enough of men telling her what she could and couldn't do and where she could and couldn't go. Now that Sammy was dead, she had a chance to start life over, but she was going to do it on her own terms.

She checked the hall to make sure the coast was clear, then woke Carlo. "Time to go, honey," she said, hoisting him onto one hip.

"Where are we going, Mama?" he asked.

"We're going to stay in a hotel. Won't that be fun?" She kept her voice to a whisper, but tried to sound excited for Carlo's sake. "They'll probably have a pool and you can go swimming."

"Will Daddy be there?"

His face was so serious—too serious for a little boy. "No, Daddy can't make it. But you and I will have a good time, won't we?" Soon, when things were more settled, she'd have to tell him about his father. Though Stacy had long ago ceased to like, much less love, her late husband, Carlo adored his daddy, even though Sammy had spent less and less time with the boy in the past months. She wasn't sure a three-year-old would understand death, but Carlo would be devastated once he accepted his father wasn't coming back. She'd postpone that pain for him a little longer.

Once in the hallway, she headed for the door marked Stairs. Less chance of running into anyone than if she risked the elevator. Fortunately, she only had to go down two floors and there was a back door. Probably where all the smokers went to sneak a cigarette, she thought, and slipped out, praying an alarm wouldn't sound.

The door opened into a parking lot at the back of the building. Only a few cars sat in the glow of overhead lights. A stiff breeze blew swirls of snow around her feet as she hurried across the concrete. She needed to find her way onto the main drag and lose herself in the crush of tourists.

She followed the sounds of voices and music to Telluride's main street, where she fell into step behind a crowd of adults and children—a big family group on vacation, she guessed. A quick check over her shoulder told her the brawny marshal wasn't following her—he was tall enough she'd have spotted him, even in this crowd. And he had the clean-cut good looks and alert attitude that pegged him as law enforcement from half a mile away.

She checked the shops along the street and spotted one that advertised children's clothing. A woman with a kid wouldn't stand out in there. She set Carlo down and pretended to look through the racks of clothing while he headed for the toy box against the wall. She needed a plan.

"Can I help you find something in particular?" an

older woman in a black wool skirt, pink blouse and boots asked.

"You have such great stuff here," Stacy gushed. "I wish I had more time to shop. I just ducked in here while I'm waiting for my husband. But I'll be back tomorrow when I have more time."

"Your son is adorable," the woman said, and she and Stacy both turned to watch Carlo fitting big foam blocks together.

"Thank you." Stacy offered her most dazzling smile. "He's going through that phase where he just loves trains and buses and airplanes. Does Telluride have a bus station?"

"Not really. Some of the hotels run shuttle buses to the airports, and there are buses to the ski area."

"Thanks. I was just curious." She could rent a car to get away, but that required a credit card and ID and would be easy to trace. She pulled out her phone and pretended to read a text. "Got to go. Come on, son, we have to go."

"But I want to stay here and play," Carlo said.

"We'll try to come back tomorrow and stay longer." She held out her hand and Carlo took it.

On the sidewalk once more, she tried to think of her next move. Maybe she could catch an airport shuttle. Anything to get out of town. She set off walking toward a high-rise on the corner where she could see several tour buses and a crowd of cars waiting for their turn to unload beneath the portico.

As she'd expected, the building was a hotel, and a busy one, crowded with people coming and going. Perfect. She'd just be one more anonymous woman in the crowd. She threaded her way through a line of tourists unloading luggage and skis from a shuttle bus and entered the lobby. She made her way to the front desk and turned on the charm for the clerk, a harried-looking young man with thinning blond hair. "What time is the airport shuttle?" she asked.

"Telluride, Montrose or Durango?" he asked, not even looking up from his computer screen.

She hesitated. "Um…"

"The bus to Durango leaves in ten minutes, but the one for Telluride will be right behind it."

"Great. Thanks." Durango it was.

She took a seat behind a potted plant and gave Carlo her phone to keep him occupied. She was showing him how to get to the games she'd downloaded for him when the phone rang, startling her.

She stared at the number. A 303 area code—Denver. Those marshals were probably based in Denver, weren't they? She hit the button to ignore the call, but a few seconds later, the chime sounded, indicating she had a message.

She hesitated, then decided to listen to the message. Maybe it wasn't the marshal at all.

Patrick Thompson's deep, velvety voice filled her ears. "Running away is not a good idea," he said. "Call me back at this number and I'll send someone to pick you up. I promise you'll be safe with us."

"Right." She was supposed to trust the people who had shot her husband. At least that was the story Thompson himself had given her. Apparently Sammy had killed his father, then turned the gun on his sister, but still, it was a federal agent who'd put the bullet in his back that killed Sammy. And though this Patrick Thompson guy had been nice enough when he was interviewing her, he was probably like all the rest—he thought she was like Sammy—a lowlife mobster, or even worse, his tramp of a wife. Why would they be so concerned about her safety? They really wanted her to tell all she knew so they could pin the Giardino family crimes on someone. But after today, no one was left to blame, except maybe for a few thugs who'd been following Sam and Sammy's orders.

She switched off the phone, hoping that would keep them from being able to trace its signal or GPS or whatever the feds used to keep tabs on people. She was tempted to leave the phone behind, but being that cut off from any resources felt too dangerous.

A deluxe passenger van pulled up and the driver announced the Durango airport shuttle. Stacy and Carlo joined the line of people climbing on board. "Name, miss?" The driver was checking off names on a list on a clipboard. He was a middle-aged man with a round face and an underdeveloped chin.

"I'm not on your list," she said. "I was hoping I could buy a ticket on board."

"I'm only supposed to take advance reservations."

Stacy shifted from foot to foot. Everyone was staring, the people behind her starting to grumble. She leaned toward the man, keeping her voice low, and at the same time giving him a look down the V-neck of her sweater—hey, she'd use whatever she had to pull this off. "Please," she said. "I just found out my mother is in the hospital and I was able to get a flight out of Durango to see her and I've got to get there. I can pay cash." And he could keep the cash and never tell anybody, if he was so inclined.

"Fifty dollars." He didn't even hesitate to bark out the sum.

She opened her purse and fished out two twenties and a ten. One thing about living with a mobster—they believed in paying cash and kept a lot around.

"Where's your luggage?" the driver asked.

"I already put it back there." She nodded toward the back of the bus, where a porter was loading suitcases.

On board the bus, she settled into a seat near the back, Carlo beside her. "Where are we going, Mama?" he asked.

"To that hotel I told you about." Once at the airport, she'd head to baggage claim and call one of the hotels that offered a free shuttle. She'd pay cash for a room and give a fake name. After dinner and a good night's sleep, she could decide what to do next.

Carlo settled with his face pressed to the glass, looking out the window. Stacy leaned her head back and closed her eyes. She was on her way. Not safe yet, but she would be soon.

"She's headed toward Durango."

Patrick leaned over the tech they'd assigned to trace Stacy's cell phone signal and studied the laptop screen and the little green dot that pinpointed her whereabouts. His last two calls to her had gone straight to voice mail, so he assumed she'd turned off her phone. Apparently she hadn't realized it still sent out a signal, even when switched off.

"What's in Durango?" Agent Sullivan asked.

"Maybe this Uncle Abel?" Stacy had said he had a ranch in Colorado, but she'd been vague about where.

"Someone else is in Durango today," Sullivan said. He held out his smartphone, which showed the front page of the Durango paper, with a story about Senator Nordley's speech to a political group in town.

Patrick's stomach churned. He'd wanted to believe Stacy's innocent victim act. Had everything she'd told them been a lie? "That's a little too convenient for coincidence," he said.

"Should we call Durango police and ask them to intercept her?" Sullivan asked.

"No. I'll go." He reached for his jacket. "I want to watch her, see what she does. And the fewer people who know about this, the better for security." He turned to the tech. "Keep tracking her. I'll stay in touch by phone."

The night was bitterly cold and blustery, big flakes of snow swirling in the parking lot security lights as he made his way to his Range Rover. He threaded the vehicle through the crowds on Main, then took the highway out of town, turning on the road up to the ski resort. This would take him over Lizard Head pass, through the small towns of Rico and Delores and into Durango. Stacy probably had a forty-minute head start on him, but he wasn't worried about following her too closely, not as long as she had her phone with her.

Provided she hadn't been smart enough to stash the phone, maybe in a bag that was now on board the shuttle while she ran the opposite direction. But he was going with his gut and the belief that she was headed to Durango herself.

He'd learned to trust his gut in his years with the U.S. Marshals, but things didn't always play out the way he wanted. Most recently, he'd agreed to allow Elizabeth Giardino, who'd been in Witness Security as Anne Gardiner, to go to the house where her father had been holed up with the rest of the family. The opportunity to catch a man on the FBI's Ten Most Wanted list after he'd been on the loose for over a year had been too tempting, especially since Elizabeth had been so determined to take the risk.

But her brother had almost killed her, and Patrick blamed himself.

He wasn't going to risk losing another woman in his care; he wouldn't let Stacy Giardino get the better of him.

When he reached the outskirts of Durango, he phoned the tech back in Telluride. "You still have her on radar?" he asked.

"Yes, sir. She was at the airport for a little bit. Then she was on the move for a bit, but she's stopped again. If you give me a moment, I can pinpoint an address."

"All right. I'll hold." He guided the car past well-lit shopping complexes down a main street lined with bars, restaurants and hotels. Like Telluride, Durango was filled with tourists celebrating after a day at the nearby ski area. It was the kind of place where it would be easy for a stranger to get lost in the crowd.

"Sir, I've got an address for you."

"Go ahead." Patrick leaned over and switched on his GPS.

The tech rattled off an address on Second Street. "I show it's a motel. Moose Head Lodge."

"Got it. Thanks." He hung up, keyed the address into his GPS then did a U-turn and headed back toward Second Street.

The Moose Head Lodge was a low-slung log-and-stone structure set back from the road. Two long wings stretched out from the central building, with doors for each room opening into the parking lot. Patrick parked the Range Rover across from the entrance and went into a lobby straight out of a Teddy Roosevelt nightmare, complete with a stuffed grizzly bear by the front counter.

"May I help you, sir?" asked the clerk, who looked scarcely old enough to shave.

"I'm looking for a young woman who just checked in. About five-two, short, pale blond hair. She probably had a little boy with her."

"I'm not allowed to give out information on our guests," he said.

"You can give me the information." Patrick flipped open his credentials on the counter.

The boy's eyes goggled. "Y-yes, sir. A woman like the one you described checked in about fifteen minutes ago. She's in Room 141—out back."

"What name did she register under?"

The boy turned to a computer and rapidly typed in some information. "She registered as Kathy Jackson. And she paid cash for her room."

"I need to reserve the closest vacant room to hers I can," Patrick said.

"That would be 142—right next door."

"I'll take it." He handed over his government credit card and filled out the reservation information.

"That room has two double beds and a microwave and minifridge," the clerk said as he handed over the card key.

"Is there someplace I can order in food?" He hadn't eaten since breakfast and it was beginning to catch up with him.

"There's a pizza place that delivers. The menu is in your room."

"That'll do." He drove the Rover around and parked in front of his room. There was no reason Stacy should recognize it, but in case she was looking out the window to see who had arrived, he kept the vehicle between him and her door and entered the room quickly.

Once inside, he made his way to the wall that separated his room from hers and pressed his ear against the sheetrock. The muffled music and voices from the television obscured any other sound at first, then he heard what he was sure was a child, and the unintelligible answer in a woman's voice.

They were there, probably in for the night, but he'd stay alert just in case. If anyone came to see her, or if she left to go out, he'd know. In the morning, he'd follow her and see where she went. Who she talked to.

He ordered pizza and listened to the sounds of splashing from the bathroom next door. Probably the boy getting a bath, but the disturbing image of Stacy in the shower drifted into his mind. Though she was petite, she had a good figure. Was he a creep for fantasizing about a woman he was supposed to protect? Or merely human for thinking about an attractive woman who was separated from him by only a wall?

And her own resistance to having anything to do

with him. Maybe her years with the Giardinos had made her wary of trusting anyone, especially those on the right side of the law. But he couldn't take the chance that some offshoot of the family—or their enemies— would come after her. The other women were in protective custody, and agents were busy tracking down everyone connected with the family and piecing together evidence for a multitude of crimes. Stacy was the only loose end at the moment.

After the pizza was delivered, he wedged the door open an inch, the better to hear any activity next door. He ate, then lay on the bed fully clothed, his weapon on the blanket beside him. All was quiet next door, even the TV silenced. He didn't expect to sleep much, if any, but he was used to long nights. He'd learned how to get through them and catch up on his rest later.

In spite of Patrick's resolve to stay awake, he must have drifted off. He woke to the sound of a woman screaming in the room next door.

Chapter Four

Instinct propelled Patrick out of bed, weapon drawn and ready. A dark sedan idled in front of the room next door, a bulky figure at the wheel. A woman's wails and the crying of a child shattered the predawn stillness and sent a jolt of adrenaline through the marshal.

He slipped out of his room, keeping to the shadows, out of reach of the parking lot lights. The door to Stacy's room stood open and just as he started to move toward it, a man ran out, Carlo clutched to his chest.

"Halt!" Patrick shouted, and shot wide, in front of the man. He didn't dare aim directly at him, too fearful of striking the child.

The kidnapper scarcely slowed as he returned fire, the shots muffled by a silencer. Patrick ducked into deeper shadow as bullets splintered the brick to his left, shards stinging the side of his face. The man tossed the boy into the backseat of the car and dived in after him and they took off, tires squealing.

Patrick fired, aiming for the vehicle's tires, but the car raced away too fast. Breathing hard, blood running down his face, he stared after the kidnappers, trying to make out the license plate number or any identifying marks on the car. But the plate had been obscured with mud, and the car was like a hundred other sedans in the city.

Heart pounding, he raced to Stacy's room. "Stacy?" he called when he reached the open doorway.

The silence that greeted him turned his blood to ice. He groped for the light switch and light illuminated chaos. The covers lay in a tangle, half off the bed, and a chair and a lamp were overturned.

"Stacy!" he called again. "It's me, Patrick Thompson. Are you all right?"

A whimper drew him to the bathroom. Weapon at the ready, he advanced toward the room. The overhead light glowed harsh on white tile and porcelain. He leaned into the doorway and found Stacy in the shower, fully clothed but slumped against the tile, blood running from a gash above her left eye. She moaned as he knelt beside her. "Stacy, can you hear me?"

She opened her eyes and stared at him, her expression blank. He knew the moment memory of all that had happened returned. Her eyes filled with tears and she struggled to stand. "Carlo! They've got Carlo!" she gasped, her voice ragged with terror and pain.

Patrick urged her back into a sitting position. "Tell me exactly what happened," he said.

"You have to go after them!" She gripped his arm, fingers digging painfully into his skin. "You have to get Carlo."

He gently pried her hand off his arm and cradled it in his own. Her fingers were ice-cold. "They drove away in a car," he said. "I promise I'll do everything I can to track them down, but I need your help. The more you can tell me, the more I'll have to use in my search."

The devastation in her eyes touched him. Gone was the cold, uncooperative woman he'd interviewed at the police station. Now she was a mother grieving for her child. She slipped her hand from his grasp and touched the cut on her head. "He hit me with the butt of his pistol."

Patrick found a washcloth and wet it from the tap, then pressed it against the gash. "Who was he? Did you recognize him?"

"No. I'm sure I never saw him before in my life. But he knew who I was. He called me Mrs. Giardino, and called Carlo by name, too."

"And you're sure you didn't know him?"

"Nothing about him was familiar, but it was dark and I was asleep when they burst in. Everything happened so fast." She slid her hand under his and took the washcloth. "What are you doing here? When did you get here?"

"I followed you here last night. I'm in the room next door."

"You were spying on me." Her eyes flashed with accusation—but that was better than the despair that had filled them seconds earlier.

"You ran away," he said. "I wanted to see where you were going. Who you talked to."

"How did you know where to find me? I didn't see anyone I knew...."

"Your phone gives off a tracking signal even when it's off." He sat back on his heels and studied her for signs she might be going into shock. But color was returning to her cheeks and she seemed more alert. "I'm surprised Sam Giardino let you have a standard phone like that."

"The men used throwaway phones, mostly, but they didn't care about the women. We weren't important enough for anyone to be concerned about where we were."

He took out his own phone. "I'll call the local police. They can put out an AMBER Alert. We might be able to stop them before they get very far."

"No!" She clutched at his arm again. "No police. He said if the police came after them they'd kill Carlo."

"If the police get to them quickly enough they won't have time to hurt the boy."

"No, please! I can't risk it. He said at the first sign of the cops they would cut Carlo's throat." She choked back a sob, struggling to keep it together. "Can't you go after them? You and I?"

"We'd have a much better chance of catching them with the police involved. An AMBER Alert will have everyone in the state looking for them."

"They'll see the notices on the news and Carlo will die!" Her voice rose, near hysterics.

He slid the phone back into his pocket. "I won't call them just yet. Tell me anything else you remember. Even little details might be important."

She nodded and scrubbed at her eyes with the back of her hands. She'd taken off her makeup, so that she looked much younger. More vulnerable.

A gentle tapping sounded on the door. "Ms. Jackson? Are you all right?" someone asked.

"I'll take care of this," Patrick said. He rose and moved quickly to the door and peered through the peephole. The desk clerk stood on the other side, looking around nervously.

Patrick opened the door. "Is something wrong?" he asked.

"Oh!" The clerk looked startled. "I, uh, I thought this was Ms. Jackson's room." He frowned at the number on the next door over—Patrick's room.

"Ms. Jackson is fine," Patrick said. "What did you need?"

"One of the guests called the front desk and said they heard gunshots coming from this room."

"They must have heard a car backfiring." The lie came easily; no need to involve this clerk until Patrick had made up his mind how to handle this.

"They sounded really certain."

"I think I'd know a gunshot, don't you?"

"Of course. Of course." He tried to see past Patrick, into the room. "And Ms. Jackson's okay?"

"She's fine. But she's not dressed for company." He winked and the clerk blushed red. No doubt the guy thought Patrick's story about conducting surveillance on Stacy had been an elaborate cover for an affair.

"I'll just, uh, get back to the front desk." The young man backed away. "If you need anything, just, uh, call."

Patrick shut the door and hooked the security chain, then returned to the bathroom. Stacy had moved from the shower to the toilet, where she sat on the closed lid, head in her hands. She looked up when he entered the room. "Who was that?"

"The front-desk clerk. Someone reported gunshots."

"What did you tell him?"

"I told him it was probably a car backfiring." He knelt in front of her. "Now tell me everything that happened."

She took a deep breath. "When I woke up, he was already in the room. He must have had a key or something, because I never heard a thing. Carlo was sleeping beside me and the guy already had hold of him, pulling him out of bed. That's what woke me."

She put the washcloth back over the gash, which had slowed its bleeding. "I screamed and he ordered me to shut up. I was terrified, finding a guy in my room like that. 'Who are you?' I asked. 'What are you doing with my son?'

"'Carlo is coming with me, Mrs. Giardino,' the guy said. 'If you know what's good for you, you won't interfere.'"

The guy might as well have told the sun not to shine. "Was there anything distinctive about his voice? An accent or anything like that?"

She frowned. "Not really. I mean, he sounded American, but not from anyplace in particular. He told me if I called the police he would kill Carlo—that if anyone followed them, they'd cut his throat." She bit her lip, fighting fresh tears.

"What did you do?" Patrick prompted.

"I tried to pull Carlo away from him. Carlo woke up and started crying. I wouldn't let go of Carlo, so the guy hit me." She winced, whether in real or remembered pain, Patrick couldn't say. "I staggered back and he grabbed me and threw me in here, then ran out with Carlo. I heard more shooting in the parking lot."

"He was firing at me. Your screaming woke me. I

tried to stop him, but he was using Carlo as a shield. I couldn't get off a good shot."

"He wore a mask," Stacy said. "A ski mask. I couldn't see his face. But his voice didn't sound familiar."

"There were two of them," Patrick said. "The driver was a big, bulky guy. The one who snatched Carlo was slighter. The car was a dark sedan with mud smeared across the license plate."

"You saw them! Then you could find them." Her eyes lit up with hope. "They won't suspect you—you're not in uniform, or driving a cop car. They probably don't even know you're here. I didn't, so why should they?"

"Except they shot at me. And I shot back."

"But they wouldn't have gotten a good look at you. Please, Patrick. Say you'll help me."

Only a colder man than him could have been immune to the pleading in her eyes. He wanted to promise her that he'd find Carlo, and soon. That he would protect them both from whoever was threatening them. He wanted to make that promise, but the knowledge that he might not be able to keep such a vow held back the words.

"Let's go back to my room and take care of that cut on your head," he said. "Then we'll decide what to do."

He found Stacy's coat and purse and draped them over her shoulders, then steadied her while she slipped into her boots. The gash had stopped bleeding and though she'd probably have a heck of a headache for a while, he hoped the damage wasn't more serious.

He led her to his room and shut the door behind them. She sat on the bed he hadn't slept in. "You'll be safer here with me," he said.

"I wasn't safe tonight. How did they find me?"

"If we can track you by your phone, they can, too."

She stared at the purse on the bed beside her. "Should I destroy the phone?"

"Not yet. The kidnappers may try to reach you through that number."

"Do they want money?" she asked. "Is that what this is about—ransom?"

"If they knew the Giardino family, they know Sam had money. Maybe they want to take advantage of his death to get their hands on some of it."

"Then maybe they won't hurt Carlo." Fresh tears filled her eyes and she covered her mouth with her hand, as if to hold back sobs.

Patrick squeezed her shoulder. "I know it's hard, but you need to pull yourself together. For Carlo's sake."

She nodded and made an effort to compose herself. He pulled out his phone again. "Who are you calling?" she asked.

"My office. I want to find out if anyone has noticed any unusual activity related to other people we're tracking in this investigation."

"You can't tell them. The kidnapper said—"

"I won't do anything I think will endanger Carlo. Why don't you go into the bathroom and clean the rest of the blood off your face while I make the call."

She glared at him, but stood and did as he asked. While she was out of the room, he'd talk to his supervisors about getting her into WITSEC right away— before the people who'd come after Carlo decided to come after her, too.

Stacy stared at herself in the hotel bathroom mirror. She looked horrible—no makeup, blood matting her hair, an ugly bruise forming above her left eye. But what did it matter, with Carlo gone? Who would have taken him? Some enemy of the Giardinos, intent on revenge? Someone after money? She closed her eyes against the pounding in her head and tried to think, but her mind offered up no answers.

She debated eavesdropping on Marshal Thompson's phone call, but she didn't really want to hear what he had to say. And she needed to stay on his good side—he was the only one who could help her find Carlo. He'd seen the men who'd taken her boy, and he had weapons and a car and she presumed some training in tracking people. She wasn't going to do better right now.

She told herself she ought to be angry he'd followed her to Durango, but if he hadn't, she'd really be stuck with no one to turn to. And he'd been a decent enough guy. He'd listened to what she'd had to say and hadn't tried to order her around as if he automatically knew what was best. That was a change from the men she was used to dealing with.

Not that he wasn't all man. A woman would have to be half-dead not to notice those broad shoulders and muscular arms. He was taller and bigger than any of the Giardino men; she felt like a shrimp next to him. But that was okay. Being around him made her feel… safe. Something she hadn't felt in a long time.

He knocked on the door as she was washing the last of the blood out of her hair. She grabbed a towel and wrapped it around her head, turban fashion, and opened the door. "What did they say?" she asked.

"They agreed we shouldn't involve the local police. It might endanger the boy and it could jeopardize our investigation."

"What investigation? You keep using that word, but what are you investigating—me?"

"Not you. In fact, I want to move you into WIT-SEC right away. When we find Carlo, we'll bring him to you."

"No."

"I know you don't like the idea, but it's the best way to protect you and—"

"No. I'm not going anywhere until we know what happened to Carlo. When you find him, I'm going to be there."

"I can't track criminals with you in tow."

"I'm not going to get in your way, and I can help."

"How can you help?"

"I know how to shoot. I know how to keep quiet and stay out of the way and most of all—I know my child. In a tense situation, he'll come to me and I can keep him calm."

His mouth remained set in that stubborn line, his gaze boring into her, but she refused to let him intimidate her. She was through with men who tried to boss her around. "I won't go into WITSEC," she said. "If you don't let me go with you, I'll search for Carlo on my own." With no car, no gun and not even a clear picture of where she was, searching on her own wasn't a choice she wanted to make, but she could steal a car, buy a gun and read a map if she had to. She'd do whatever it took to find her boy.

"My first job is to protect you."

"Then you can do that by taking me with you to look for Carlo. Now come on. We're wasting time talking about it. We need to go after them."

She tried to push past him, but he stopped her, one hand on her shoulder. "You can't go out with wet hair. You'll freeze."

She pulled the towel from her head. "I don't care about my hair. It can dry in the car."

"You won't be any good to Carlo, or to me, if you catch pneumonia."

"Fine." She turned and grabbed the hair dryer that hung by the sink. "But as soon as my hair is dry, we leave."

She expected him to leave her to the task, but he remained in the doorway, reflected in the mirror, his gaze fixed on her. She tried to ignore him, but that was impossible; even if the mirror hadn't been there, she could feel his eyes on her, sense his big, brooding presence just over her shoulder. Why had he said that, about her not being any good to him if she got sick? Did he really think she was such as important witness in his mysterious "investigation"? He certainly didn't need her any other way.

Except maybe in the way men always seemed to need women, a traitorous voice in her head whispered. She shifted against an uncomfortable tightness in her lower abdomen, an awareness of herself not as mother, wife or daughter, but as a young, desirable woman. She'd buried that side of herself when she married Sammy Giardino—that it should resurface now astounded her. She'd heard of people who reacted to stress in inappropriate ways, for instance, by laughing at funerals. Was her response to tragedy and peril going to be this odd state of semiarousal? She couldn't think of anything less appropriate, especially if she was getting turned on by some big brute of a cop.

She switched off the hair dryer and whirled to face him. "What are you staring at?" she asked.

She expected him to say something about her looks—to tell her she was pretty or sexy or a similar come-on. It was the sort of thing men always said, especially when they wanted to talk you into their bed. Instead, he straightened and uncrossed his arms. "I was thinking how wrong the Giardinos were to take you for granted," he said, then, not waiting for an answer, he turned away.

She stared after him, confusion and pleasure warring in her. What some cop thought of her shouldn't matter, but she wasn't used to compliments—if, indeed, he'd meant the comment to be flattering. The fact that he saw past her physical presence to something in her character left her feeling off balance. She was used to people taking her for granted—not mattering to others was a kind of camouflage. It kept you safe. For this man to really see who she was past her skin felt daring and dangerous.

"Are you coming?" he called.

"Yes!" She grabbed up her coat and purse and followed him across the parking lot to his car—a black SUV that looked like something a rich tourist would drive, not a federal agent. If Carlo's kidnappers saw this vehicle behind them, they wouldn't be suspicious.

"Don't get your hopes up that this is going to work," he said as she buckled her seat belt. "If these guys are pros, they've already switched cars and headed out of town."

"But maybe they didn't," she said. "There isn't much traffic this time of night. Maybe we'll see them. They don't expect anyone to come after them, so maybe they'll be careless."

"That's a lot of maybes." He started the engine and put the vehicle in gear. "But criminals have done dumber things."

They turned onto the dark, deserted street and headed toward the highway. Streetlights shone on dirty snowbanks pushed up on the side of the road. They passed few cars; Stacy studied each one closely, but none contained anyone who looked like the man who had attacked her and taken Carlo.

They drove to the edge of town, then turned back and headed in the opposite direction. Patrick turned into a motel parking lot. "Look for a black sedan with mud on the plates," he said. "It's a long shot, but they may have holed up somewhere close."

Scarcely daring to breathe, she leaned close to the window and studied each vehicle they passed: old trucks, new SUVs, brightly colored sports cars. But no black sedan.

They checked four more motels with the same results. Patrick cruised through a silent shopping center. "I think they've left town," he said.

Profound weariness dragged at her. If she closed her eyes, she might fall asleep sitting up. Yet how could she sleep when Carlo was out there, frightened, held captive by strangers? "What do we do now?" she asked.

"We need a plan." He turned the car back toward their motel. "And we need more clues."

She took out her phone and stared at it, willing it to

ring. "If they'd just call and tell us what they want," she said.

"Maybe all they wanted was Carlo."

Carlo was all she wanted, too. He was all she had in this world. She couldn't accept that he'd disappear from her life this way. "He has to be out there somewhere," she said.

Patrick didn't answer. In the blue-white light of street lamps he looked grim and forbidding, shadows beneath his eyes and the golden glint of beard across his jaw. He looked like a man who wouldn't give up. She held on to that hope like a lifeline in a pitch-black sea.

Back at the hotel, she sank onto the edge of the bed. Her head throbbed and her eyes were scratchy from crying, but the physical discomfort was nothing compared with the pain of missing Carlo and feeling so helpless to do anything to protect him. "I'm going to look next door," Patrick said. "See if I can spot any clues. I'll need your key."

She fished the card from her purse, but didn't release her hold on it when he reached for it. "Give me your key," she said. "I'm going to the lobby for a soda. There's a vending machine there." The drink might settle her stomach and help her feel more alert.

They exchanged keys and she followed him out the door and walked past her room to the lobby. She kept out of view of the desk clerk, not wanting to explain the gash on her head, and found the vending machines in a back hallway. A handful of quarters later, she held a can of diet cola and a regular cola. Patrick didn't strike her as the diet type, but he'd probably appreciate the caffeine as much as she did.

Outside once more, she shivered in the cold that seemed to sink into her bones, despite the ski parka she hugged around herself. The parking lot was quiet and profoundly silent. Her footsteps on the concrete echoed in the stillness. The rooms she passed were dark and silent, as well. She and Patrick might have been the only ones here.

She hunched her shoulders and increased her pace. The sooner she was back with Patrick, the better she'd feel. And maybe he'd found something in her room that would lead them to Carlo.

She turned the corner of the building and strong arms grabbed her from behind. A man's thick fingers clamped over her mouth and a sharp blade pricked at her throat. "Make a sound and you're dead."

Chapter Five

The scent of Stacy's perfume—something expensive and floral—lingered in her hotel room. Patrick stood in the doorway and surveyed the scene, searching for anything that might provide a clue as to the identity of Carlo's kidnappers. The double bed still bore the indentations where mother and son had slept, and a single strand of white-blond hair glinted on the pillow. Patrick studied the hair and thought of the woman who had left it behind—such a compelling mix of strength and frailty, reserve and openness. She refused to cooperate in letting him protect her, and that only served to make him more determined to keep her from harm.

He turned away from the bed and examined the dull-brown carpeting, which was worn and matted, especially in front of the door. But a fresh smear of mud caught his eye. He knelt and with the tip of a pen, pried up a quarter-size fragment of the still-pliable clay. He sniffed it and caught the definite odor of manure—from horses? Cows?

He found an envelope in the desk drawer and slid the mud sample inside. He could have someone analyze it to narrow down the probable source, but dirt alone wouldn't be enough to find a man who didn't want to be found.

He searched the rest of the room and the bathroom and closet and came up empty-handed. Stacy had come here with nothing but the clothes on her back. What had she planned to do? Where would she have gone from here?

He would ask her, but he doubted she'd tell him. She definitely kept things to herself. *I know how to keep quiet and stay out of the way,* she'd said. Is that how she'd survived in the Giardino household—by being invisible? He'd known women like that, who suppressed every opinion and action and feeling in order to survive living with an abuser. In the end, they almost always ended up hurt anyway. Anger flared at the thought that Stacy had been forced to live that way.

He left the room, closing the door quietly behind him. He was turning toward his own room when a muffled sound made the hair on the back of his neck stand up. He waited and the sound came again, very faint, from up the walkway and around the corner.

The rough brick of the building scraped against his jacket as he flattened himself against it, his gun drawn and held upright against his chest. He moved sideways, one silent step at a time, toward the corner. A quick glance down this side of the motel revealed nothing incriminating. Then he spotted the darkened niche that held trash cans and a fire extinguisher. Nothing moved within that shadowed space, yet his heart raced in warning. He cocked his weapon, then slid a mini Maglite from his pocket and directed the beam into the darkest recesses of the alcove.

And into the terrified eyes of Stacy.

"Drop the gun or she's dead!" barked a man's voice.

Patrick carefully uncocked the weapon and let it fall to the sidewalk. "Who are you?" he asked. "What do you want?"

A man, middle-aged and bulky with muscle and layers of clothing, moved out of the niche, dragging Stacy with him. Her gray eyes were wide with fright, all color drained from her face. But the bright red blood that beaded where the blade of her captor's knife met her neck stood out against her pale skin. The wound made Patrick see red of a different kind, and he sucked in a deep breath, forcing himself to maintain calm.

"Stay there," the bulky man ordered. "My friend will be along in a minute to take care of you."

Patrick ignored the threat. Whether it was real or not, he needed to focus on the man in front of him and learn all he could about him in order to know how to defeat him. This guy didn't look like the one who'd taken Carlo; he was shorter and stockier. He wore dark slacks and a black overcoat and a stocking cap, but no mask.

"Where are you taking me?" Stacy asked, her voice quavering.

"Shut up!" the man said, and a fresh trickle of blood leaked from beneath the blade of the knife.

Stacy's eyes widened, but she kept talking. "Are you taking me to Carlo?" she asked. "If you're taking me to my son, I'll go willingly."

"My boss wants to see you." Like too many people, Stacy's captor apparently couldn't follow his own advice about keeping quiet.

"Who is your boss?" Patrick asked.

"One more word out of you and I cut her throat." He jerked Stacy more tightly against him and she gasped. Her eyes widened again, but not in pain this time. Patrick whirled around in time to see a second, thinner man move toward him. His knees slammed into the concrete walkway as he dropped to the ground and air reverberated with the sound of the shots that sailed over his head.

Stacy screamed and fought wildly against the man who held her. Patrick was torn between trying to save her and dealing with the second man, who had lowered his weapon to fire again. Stacy distracted them both as her heel connected hard with the stocky man's kneecap and sent him reeling. Patrick dived for his gun, rolled and came up firing as the second man let loose another volley of shots. The man fell back, shot in the chest, and Patrick leaped to his feet and pointed his weapon at the stocky man.

But Stacy's attacker was already running away across the parking lot. Patrick took off after him, pounding across the pavement, but the stocky man's bulk was deceiving; he quickly outpaced the marshal and was swallowed up in darkness.

Breathing hard from the exertion and the altitude, Patrick returned to Stacy. She stood with one hand to her throat, staring down at the wounded man, who lay inert, blood seeping from the chest wound. "Are you all right?" Patrick touched her shoulder and looked into her eyes. Some of the terror had receded, replaced by the weariness of someone who had seen too much to process.

"I'm okay." She took a deep breath. "I don't know about him, though." She indicated the man on the ground.

Patrick knelt beside him. "Who sent you?" he asked.

The man gave no answer; he appeared unconscious.

"I've called 911." The desk clerk, wide-eyed and breathless, raced up to them. "I heard the shots." He gaped at the man on the ground. "Who is he? Is he dead?"

Patrick searched the man's pockets and found a wallet and a driver's license. "This says his name is Nathan Forest."

"What happened?" The clerk turned to Stacy. "You're bleeding! I should have asked for an ambulance."

Patrick replaced Forest's wallet and stood. "This man and his companion tried to mug Ms. Jackson." He took Stacy's arm. "We'd better go."

She nodded, and didn't try to pull away when he turned her toward his room.

"Shouldn't you wait for the police?" the clerk asked.

"You can tell them everything they need to know." Patrick hurried with Stacy down the walkway and into his room, where he shut and locked the door. Then he led her into the brightly lit bathroom. "Tip your head back and let me have a look," he said, one finger under her chin.

She winced with the effort, but lifted her chin and let him examine the wound. "I imagine it hurts, but it's not very deep," he said. He grabbed a hand towel from a stack by the sink and handed it to her. "Put that around your neck to stop the bleeding, and then we've got to get out of here before the police show up. They'll ask a lot of questions we don't want to answer right now."

She pressed the towel to her neck. "Thank you," she said.

"For what?"

"For not involving the police."

"I'll have someone from my office contact them to see if they learn anything about Forest and his companion, but for now I don't want to waste any time with them. Get your things and let's go."

They passed the police cruiser and the ambulance on their way out of the parking lot. Stacy, the bloody towel in her lap, watched over her shoulder until the motel was out of sight, then faced forward once more. "Neither one of those men looked like the man who took Carlo," she said.

"I didn't think so, either," he said.

"So who were they? What did they want?"

He checked the mirror. So far, so good. They weren't being followed. "Two possibilities come to mind," he said. "Carlo was too much to handle, so whoever orchestrated the first kidnapping sent those two to get you."

"Then I would have gone with them. I could have helped Carlo."

"The other possibility is that the first two guys screwed up. They weren't supposed to leave you behind as a witness, so these two were supposed to finish the job."

She sucked in her breath and touched the cut on her neck. "What are we going to do now?"

"We need to find another place to stay. We need sleep and a shower and you need to take care of your wounds."

"I can't sleep, not when I could be out looking for Carlo."

"You can't help him if you're half-dead on your feet.

And we aren't going to find anything wandering around in the dark. Tomorrow morning we'll start fresh. I'm going to call my office and arrange to get another car. The desk clerk will tell the local police about this one and they'll probably be looking for it, to talk to us about Nathan Forest."

"I'll bet that's not his real name."

She was smart enough to figure that out, at least. "Nathan Bedford Forest was a Confederate general during the Civil War," he said. "Maybe this guy's mother or father was a history buff."

"Or maybe he made it up."

"Probably he made it up."

"And after we get a new car?"

"I think we'd better go see your Uncle Abel and find out if he knows anything about what's going on."

"Uncle Abel? Do you think he's behind this?"

"He's the closest living relative to Sam Giardino— the one Sam threatened to put in charge of the family business. And didn't you say he has a ranch somewhere around here?"

"Crested Butte. Do you think he has Carlo? Or knows who does?"

"The man who took Carlo had mud on his shoes— mud mixed with manure. The kind of thing you'd find on a ranch."

"But that could be anywhere—it doesn't have to be Abel's ranch."

"You're right. But it's the only clue we have right now. Talking to Abel seems a good place to start. If he doesn't know anything, maybe he can tell us who would be interested in the boy. You said Sam threatened to pass the family business on to Abel?"

"I don't think he was serious. Everyone always said the two brothers weren't on good terms."

"They might have patched up their differences and been in touch recently. Maybe that's why Sam decided to vacation in Colorado."

"Maybe." She sounded doubtful. "What if Abel doesn't know anything?"

"We'll worry about that when the time comes."

STACY WAS WORN out with worry by the time Patrick located a motel he thought suitable for their purposes. Set back from the road on a side street, the collection of 1950s-era cabins strung together in a row offered rooms for rent by the week and free local phone calls. "There's a light in the office, so we should be able to get a room," Patrick said as he cruised past the place. "I'll park the car a few blocks away and we'll walk back."

"Why do we have to do that?" she protested. The thought of walking even a few hundred yards in the dark and cold made her want to sink down into the seat and refuse to move.

"If the police spot the car, I don't want to make it easy for them to find us."

In the end, she made the walk leaning on Patrick. When he'd offered his support her first instinct had been to refuse, but she was so tired she was almost dizzy, and his arm around her was the only thing that felt safe and solid in the world.

Their room was cold and musty, with two double beds covered with green chenille spreads, and the kind of maple furniture Stacy remembered from visits to her grandmother's house when she was a little girl. She stretched out on the bed farthest from the door while Patrick made phone calls.

Though she would have sworn she was too worried to sleep, she was unconscious within seconds, despite the glare of the overhead light and the low murmur of Patrick's voice across the room. She woke some time later to darkness, and the sensation of someone slipping her boots from her feet, then tucking a blanket around her. She opened her eyes and stared up at Patrick. "I didn't want to wake you," he said, and settled the blanket around her shoulders.

She struggled back to consciousness. "What did your office say? Do they know anything about Nathan Forest?"

"Nothing yet. They're going to send someone with a new car for us. In the meantime, go back to sleep."

"You won't leave, will you?" Where had that question come from? She'd never wanted this lawman in her life, but now, with Carlo missing and after being attacked twice in one night by strangers, the thought of being left alone terrified her.

"No, I won't leave." He patted her shoulder. "I'm going to lie down in the other bed and try to get some sleep. You do the same."

"All right." But welcome oblivion didn't return easily. She lay in the darkness, listening to the hum and tick of the heater, and the creak of bedsprings as Patrick shifted on his own mattress. He definitely wasn't like any lawman she'd ever encountered—not that she'd known many. Along with the rest of the family, she'd attended Sam Giardino's trial a year and a half ago and seen the officers who surrounded him—cool, expressionless men and women in uniform who never glanced her way. She'd never bothered to differentiate one from the other. They were all simply "the law." The enemies of the Giardino family, and thus her enemies, too.

Patrick had that same erect bearing and devotion to duty. He'd regarded her with suspicion from the moment he found her hiding in the basement, and he'd followed her to Durango because he suspected her of some wrongdoing, she was sure.

But he'd also risked his own life to protect her, and he'd ignored at least some of the law to help search for Carlo without involving the local police. She was a stranger to him, yet he acted like he cared. Did he think she was such a valuable witness for his mysterious case, or was something else at work here?

Sleep finally overtook her, though she slept fitfully, haunted by dreams of shadowy figures who pursued her and glimpses of Carlo reaching for her, calling for her, his little face streaked with tears.

"Stacy, wake up. It's all right. You're safe."

She woke sobbing, the pillowcase wet from her tears. In the dim glow from the bedside lamp, she stared at Patrick. He'd removed his shirt, belt and shoes, and sat on the side of the bed dressed only in slacks. Light glinted on the dusting of hair across his muscular chest. Such an odd thing to notice at a time like this, she thought. It was such an intimate, masculine detail—maybe her mind's attempt to avoid thinking about the bad dreams, or the reality that her son had been taken from her.

"You had a bad dream," he said, one hand resting warm and heavy on her shoulder.

"I was dreaming of Carlo." Her voice broke, and she closed her eyes in a futile effort to hold back more tears.

"I really don't think the people who took him will hurt him," he said.

"How can you say that? I read in the paper about children who are kidnapped and suffer horrible things." She pressed her hand to her mouth to stop the words, though she couldn't keep back the thoughts behind them.

"This doesn't feel like that kind of crime," he said. "They wanted Carlo specifically, and I think they want him alive and unharmed."

"You can't know that," she said.

"No. But I have good instincts about these things."

She wanted to believe him. He sounded so calm and certain. So reassuring. "I'm scared to go back to sleep," she said. "Scared of the dreams."

"You need to rest." He looked at the clock beside the bed. It showed 3:19 a.m., though it seemed days since she'd gotten off the bus in Durango. So much had happened.

He reached to turn off the light again and she grabbed his wrist. "Please."

"You want me to leave the light on?"

With the light on the chances of either one of them getting more sleep would be less. And she needed him alert and ready for action tomorrow. Or later today, actually. But the thought of facing the darkness again unsettled her. "Maybe you could just…lie here beside me." She looked away as she spoke. He probably thought she was trying to come on to him; men always thought that. "Just lie here, nothing else," she added. "I'd feel safer that way."

He looked past her to the pillow on the other side of the bed. "All right." He got up and walked around the bed, then stretched out on top of the covers. "Will you cut the light out now?" he asked.

She reached up and switched off the lamp. The weight of his body made the mattress dip toward him. If she relaxed even a little, she'd probably slide down toward him. "You should get a blanket," she said. "You'll be cold."

He reached over and pulled the spread from the bed closest to the door. "I'll be fine now," he said. "Get some sleep."

She closed her eyes and tried to do as he'd said, but the awareness of him next to her kept her tense. She lay rigid, trying not to move or breathe, waiting for morning.

"What's wrong?" he asked, long after she was sure he'd fallen asleep.

You're what's wrong, she could have said. *I want you here and I don't want you here.* "I don't know," she said. "So much has happened."

"You've been through a lot," he said. "Too much."

"How do you deal with it?" she asked. "I mean, people shooting at you. Having to shoot other people."

"I try to stay focused on what's important."

"What's important," she repeated. Carlo was the only thing that was really important to her. "Do you have a family? Kids?" She knew so little about him.

"No family. No kids. My parents are still alive, but they retired to Florida. I don't see them a lot."

"So it's just you."

"I have a sister. She's in Denver, so I see her as much as I can."

"That's nice." She'd always wanted a sister or brother, someone who knew her and all about her life and loved her anyway. Unconditionally. At least, that was what she imagined having a sibling would be like. "No girl-friend?" She wished she could take the question back as soon as she asked it. She didn't want him thinking she was interested in him that way, not with him lying next to her in bed like this.

He was silent a long moment before answering. "This kind of job is hard on relationships."

"Life is hard on relationships." At least, the life she knew. Her parents had been together for years, but that was more out of stubbornness than anything else. The Giardinos stayed together because divorce was danger-ous. Sammy had made it clear that if she tried to leave him she would lose everything—the money, Carlo and even her life.

She squeezed her eyes shut. She didn't want to think about Sammy or the Giardinos. She needed to stay fo-cused on the present. Right here. Right now. Talking to Patrick was calming her down. She felt as if she could say anything to him here in the dark, knowing he was close, but not touching him. Not seeing his face to read whether he was judging her or not. Just laying it all out there. "Do you ever get lonely?" she asked.

"All the time."

"Yeah." She licked her lips, tasting the salt from her tears. "Me, too."

She gave up resisting then and let her body slide toward his. She lay alongside him, and rested her head in the hollow of his shoulder. He stiffened. "What are you doing?"

"Nothing," she said. "Just…hold me. That's all."

Gradually, he relaxed, and brought his arm up to cradle her close. "I just…don't want to feel so alone right now," she said. "Don't make a big deal out of it or anything."

She was prepared for him to argue, or to try to take advantage. If that happened, she'd have to move away. But he merely let out a long breath. "All right," he said. "Get some sleep."

But she was already sinking under, lulled by his warmth and strength, and the sensation that here was a man who could protect her, the way no man ever had.

Chapter Six

Patrick woke from restless sleep, aroused and all-too-aware of the woman nestled against him. Though Stacy was fully dressed, the soft fullness of her breast pressed against his side, and her hand, palm down, lay on his stomach, tantalizingly close to the erection that all but begged for her attention.

A lesser man—one who didn't have the job of protecting a witness in a federal case and tracking down her missing child—might have taken advantage of the situation. He could have rolled over and pulled her close and sought comfort and release for both of them in the act of lovemaking.

But even if Stacy Giardino had been open to the idea of sex with him—and considering her wariness of him the day before, that was doubtful—she was off-limits to him. She was his responsibility and his duty, not a potential lover.

Reminding himself of this didn't do a lot to quell his desire, but it enabled him to ease himself away from her and out of bed. He pulled on his shirt, then checked his phone on the way to the bathroom. A text from his office informed him a four-wheel-drive Jeep had been left for him in the parking lot, the keys under the driver's-side floor mat. Someone had picked up his other car from its parking place two blocks over, along with the sample of mud from Stacy's hotel room that he'd left on the backseat.

A second text informed him that Nathan Forest had died before regaining consciousness. So far nothing new had surfaced about his identity or his connections.

The bedsprings creaked as he stepped out of the bathroom and Stacy let out a soft moan. He moved to the side of the bed. "Stacy?" he asked softly.

She blinked up at him, confusion quickly replaced by the pain of remembering all that had happened. He tensed, prepared for her to break down, but she pulled herself together and shoved herself into a sitting position. "Have you heard any news?" she asked.

"We have a new car and Nathan Forest is dead. Nothing more."

She covered her eyes with one hand. The gash on her forehead was bruised around the edges, but it didn't look infected. She probably should have had stitches to prevent a scar, but it was too late for that now. The cuts on her neck glowed pink against the pale skin. "How are you feeling?" he asked.

"Everything hurts." She uncovered her eyes and looked around the room. "Is there coffee?"

A two-cup coffeemaker and supplies sat on a tray by the television. "I'll make some," he said. "Why don't you take a shower?"

"Good idea." She moved past him to the bathroom and a few seconds later he heard the water running. He started the coffee, then slipped out to the car.

The Jeep was several years old, the red paint faded

and the leather seats worn. But it was equipped with a new GPS and good tires. And in the backseat he found two plastic shopping bags filled with toiletries, snacks and a change of clothes for each of them. Somebody at headquarters deserved a commendation for that.

He carried the bags inside and tapped on the bathroom door. "Stacy, I've got a bag here with some clothes and other things for you," he said.

No answer. Maybe she couldn't hear him for the shower.

He tried the knob. The door wasn't locked. He eased the door open, keeping his eyes averted from the steaming shower, and set the bag just inside the door, then went to pour himself a cup of coffee and wait.

When she emerged from the bathroom half an hour later, damp hair curling around her face and smelling of floral soap, he was seated on the end of the bed, the television on and turned to the local news. "I've never been so grateful for clean underwear and toothpaste in my life," she said. "Where did they come from?"

"The agent who delivered the new car left them."

"Well, he—or she—deserves a raise." She smoothed a hand over the pink-and-white hoodie and matching yoga pants. "I'm betting it's a woman with good taste. She even thought to include a little face powder and lipstick. I feel almost human again."

She definitely looked like she was feeling better. The dark circles beneath her eyes had faded some, and she'd combed her hair to hide most of the gash on her forehead. In the casual clothing, with the lighter makeup, she looked younger and more vulnerable than she had when he'd first questioned her the day before.

He stood and rubbed his hand across the bristles on his chin. "I think I'll shower and shave," he said. "There are some snacks in that other bag there. Help yourself to breakfast."

She glanced at the television. "Any news?"

"Nothing of interest to us."

After a shower and shave, he dressed in the Nordic sweater and jeans he found in the bag and returned to the bedroom. The casual clothing made him and Stacy look more like tourists, or even locals. Stacy sat cross-legged on the end of the bed, eating peanut-butter crackers and staring at the television. "They just did a promo about a shootout at a Durango hotel last night," she said. "I think that's us."

He sat beside her and waited through commercials for a used-car dealer, life insurance and dish detergent. Then a somber-faced reporter came on to report on an exclusive break in the story of a shooting at a local hotel. "Though the incident was at first reported to be a random mugging, we've since learned information that ties this killing to organized crime. The woman assaulted, who has since disappeared, was Stacy Giardino, daughter-in-law of fugitive Sam Giardino, head of one of the country's deadliest organized crime families, who was gunned down at a vacation home near Telluride yesterday morning. Ms. Giardino was accompanied by a man who identified himself as a U.S. Marshal. The two left the hotel shortly after the shooting before local police could question them. If you see either Ms. Giardino or her companion, please contact police immediately."

The reporter described Patrick as two inches shorter

than his true height, with brown hair. The screen then flashed a photograph of Stacy that had been taken at her wedding, almost five years before. She'd worn her hair long then and looked all of sixteen, swallowed up in yards of billowing tulle and satin.

Patrick punched the remote to turn off the television. "I don't think we have to worry about anyone tracking us down based on that description, but we shouldn't take any chances."

"How did they figure out who we are?" she asked. "I registered at the hotel under a fake name."

"I used my real name," Patrick said. "And I showed the clerk my U.S. Marshal's ID. He probably gave that information to police and someone made the connection to Sam Giardino. Nothing is really secret anymore."

"What are we going to do?" she asked.

"Keep moving and try not to attract attention."

"I'm ready to leave now." She stood and brushed crumbs from her lap. "You said we were going to Uncle Abel's ranch?"

"That's the plan. Do you know where it is?"

She shook her head. "Just Crested Butte. I don't think the town's that big. Maybe we could ask?"

"We could, but we'll have to be careful. We don't want to let them know we're on their trail, if they have Carlo."

"Do you think they do?"

"I don't know. But it's the only direction I can think to go at the moment. I asked my office to look for an Abel Giardino in Crested Butte, but they haven't turned up anything yet."

"Maybe he's using another name. The family story

was always that he didn't want anything to do with the business."

"That could be. I think the best thing for us to do now is to go to the town and see what we can find out."

"How long will it take us to get there?" she asked.

"About five hours, if the weather cooperates."

She glanced out the window. "It's gray out there, but it's not actually snowing."

"We should be fine. Come on."

They carried the supplies and their dirty clothes with them, not wanting to leave behind anything the authorities—or their enemies—could use to track them. Though not as comfortable as his Rover, the Jeep ran well, and the heater worked, blasting out heat to cut the frigid outside temperature.

They soon reached the outskirts of town and drove past empty snow-covered fields and expanses of evergreen woods and rocky outcroppings. Occasionally one or two houses sat back from the road, or small herds of horses or cattle gathered around hay that had been spread for them. "How do people live out here?" Stacy asked. "It's so remote."

"It is, but maybe you and I think that because we're city people."

"Where are you from?" she asked.

"New York. I grew up in Queens, just like you."

She hugged her arms across her chest. "I don't know if I like that you know so much about me. I'm not a criminal, you know. I've never had so much as a parking ticket."

"I know." At least, she hadn't actively participated

in any crimes that he knew of. "But you married into a criminal family."

"So that makes me guilty by association?"

"In a way, it does." Innocent, law-abiding people didn't have intimate connections to mob criminals, in his experience.

"Was that why you followed me to Durango? Because you thought I was going to commit a crime?"

"I wondered why you were running away from the protection we offered. I wanted to see what you would do."

"You call it protection—I call it another form of prison." She looked away. "I've had enough of that, thank you."

"Are you saying you were a prisoner of the Giardinos?"

"I might as well have been. I promised 'til death do us part, and Sammy made it clear I had to keep that promise."

"You told me your father and his father arranged the marriage, but you never told me why you agreed to it."

"My father owed Sam Giardino some kind of debt. I don't know what it was, but he made it clear that I had to marry Sammy in order to save his life."

So a wife for Sammy was the price for George Franklin's safety? From what Patrick knew of Sam Giardino, this kind of twisted plan was his specialty. "How old were you?"

"I was nineteen. I had a dead-end job at a boutique in the mall, but I wanted to go to college. I knew the Giardinos had money. I figured I'd marry Sammy, save my dad, go to school on Sammy's dime and divorce him after a few years. But it didn't work out that way."

The regret in her voice pulled at him. "No divorce."

"And no school. Sam thought educating women was a waste of money and what he said was the law. So Sammy went to law school and I read his books and wrote his papers."

"And you had Carlo."

"Yes." She picked at imaginary lint on her pants. "I love him more than anything, and I'm so glad I have him now, but I wasn't thrilled about becoming pregnant so quickly. Of course, by then I'd figured out that even without a kid, the Giardinos weren't going to let me leave. Once Carlo came along, I was really stuck."

"What will you do now that Sammy is dead?"

"I'd like to go back to school, if I can scrape up the money. I'll get a job, find a place to live. I figure after helping Sammy through law school getting my own law degree won't be too hard."

Simple dreams. Not the plans of a criminal mind. Of course, some criminals were very good actors. They could make people believe what they wanted them to. But he didn't think Stacy fell into that category. "What kind of law?"

"I don't know. I'd like to do something to help women and children."

"You'd make a good lawyer."

"You really think so?"

"You're calm under pressure. You're smart and you know how to think on your feet."

"Thanks. I really fooled you, because I don't feel

calm." She twisted her hands together. "Do you think we'll find Carlo?"

"We'll find him." He tightened his fingers around the steering wheel. He would get the boy back to his mother if it was the last thing he did.

The strains of an Alicia Keys song drifted up from the floorboards. Stacy stared at him, the color drained from her face. "My phone."

"Answer it." He pulled over to the side of the road, but left the engine running.

She fumbled in her purse and pulled out the phone. "Hello?"

"Put it on speaker," he said.

She did so, and a woman's soft, deep voice filled the Jeep. "Hello, Stacy."

"Who is this?"

"That's not important. But unless you want your son's death on your hands, you'll turn around now and go back to Durango or New York or Timbuktu, for all I care. Do that, and we'll let you both live. Keep on the course you're on and we'll kill the boy and then come after you again. And this time, you won't escape."

"Who are you? What have you done with my son?" She raised her voice. "Carlo, are you there? Can you hear me? It's Mommy."

"Mommy! Mommy, where are you? I'm scared. Mommy!"

The phone went dead. Stacy covered her mouth with one hand and stared at the phone.

Patrick gently pried the phone from her hand and scrolled back to the history. "Unknown number," he said. "I could try to have someone trace it, but they were probably smart enough to make the call from a throwaway phone, or even a pay phone. There's still a few of those around."

"What are we going to do?" Her voice shook, but she was holding it together. After hearing her son's voice in distress, that took a lot of guts. His job was to stay calm and make it as easy as he could for her.

"First, we get rid of the phone." He slid the cover off the back and popped out the SIM chip, dropped it to the floor of the Jeep and smashed it with his heel. Then he broke the rest of the phone into as many pieces as he could and tossed them out the window.

"You can't just throw them out the window," she protested.

"I'm sorry, but we can't risk keeping the phone when someone can use it to trace you."

"No, I mean, you're littering."

She looked so genuinely distressed, he bit back his laughter. "I'll write myself a ticket later. Come on. We have to get out of here." He put the Jeep in gear and made a U-turn, headed back the way they'd come.

STILL REELING FROM hearing Carlo crying for her, Stacy struggled to understand what was happening. "What are you doing?" she asked Patrick. "Where are you going?" Surely he wasn't giving up the plan to go to Crested Butte.

"That was in case anyone was watching. I want them to think we're acting on their threat and retreating. I looked at the map while you were in the shower this morning and we can get to Crested Butte another way, using back roads."

She sat back, though truly relaxing was impossible. Carlo had sounded so upset.... She swallowed a knot of tears. She couldn't break down now. She had to keep it together, for her little boy's sake.

Patrick patted her arm—though whether this was a gesture of reassurance or merely to get her attention, she wasn't sure. "Did you recognize the woman's voice?" he asked.

"No." There had been nothing familiar about the voice at all.

"Is Abel married?"

"He wasn't the last time I saw him, but that was five years ago."

"He was living with his mother then."

"Yes. And she didn't sound like that. She was old."

"How old?"

"Seventies? Abel is fifty, at least. Maybe we're on the wrong track." This new idea increased her agitation. "Maybe Abel doesn't have anything to do with this and we're wasting time, while whoever does have Carlo gets farther and farther away."

"That's possible. But whoever has him knew—probably from your phone—that we'd left Durango and were headed toward Crested Butte. And they wanted you to go away. That tells me we're headed in exactly the right direction."

"What if they do have someone watching us and he—or she—figures out we didn't really turn around?" She looked around, as if expecting to see someone spying on them. "They might hurt Carlo."

"I don't think so. They took the boy on purpose, for a specific reason. If they'd wanted to kill him, they could have done away with both of you in your hotel room before either of you woke up. They're making these threats to scare you and keep you away, but I think they want the boy alive."

"But why would they want him? He's just a baby." Her voice trembled on these last words, but she sucked in a deep breath and continued. "He can't tell them anything or give them anything."

"What about Sam Giardino's will? Does Carlo inherit anything now that Sammy is dead, too?"

"You'd know the answer to that better than I do. Doesn't the government confiscate ill-gotten gains?"

"If they can prove a link to a crime, yes."

"It's not as if Sammy had tons of cash and money in bank accounts. He lived well, but most of his money was in the business. And Elizabeth is still alive. She's bound to inherit something."

"But the majority would go to his son, or his son's son, I would think."

"Yeah. Sam was a chauvinist, all right. Though he'd have said he was following tradition." Women didn't rate as high as the family dog in the Giardino household. "But even if Sam had decided to leave his money to Carlo, he wouldn't just hand everything over to a three-year-old," she said. "There'd be a trust or something to tie the money up until Carlo was old enough to take control."

"Then maybe money isn't the driving force here. What else?"

"I can't think of any reason why anyone would want to take Carlo." He was her baby. No one loved him or cared for him more than she did—why would anyone else even notice him?

"I think this is our turnoff up here," he said, indicating a road that branched to the left. "It goes around the lake and doesn't get much use this time of year, but it's usually kept plowed."

"I'll take your word for it," she said.

The two-lane road was paved for the first mile, and then blacktop gave way to gravel. A thin layer of snow covered the rock, and banks of snow had been pushed up on either side. He had to slow his speed to about thirty around the many curves; no doubt it would take even longer to get to Crested Butte. She struggled to avoid fidgeting with impatience.

"I still can't believe anyone would want anything from Carlo," she said after half an hour of silence. Talking was better than letting her thoughts range out of control, and for a guy, Patrick was a decent listener. He didn't discount her ideas with every breath.

"Maybe we're looking at this wrong," Patrick said. "Maybe Carlo isn't the target at all—maybe it's you."

"Me?"

"If someone wanted to hurt you, what better way to do that than to take away the one person who matters most to you?"

She wrapped her arms across her stomach, his words like a physical blow. "If Sammy was still alive, I might believe he'd do something like this. He hated me enough."

"Why did he hate you?"

She'd spent most of her marriage trying to figure out the answer to that question. "I was one more thing his father forced on him. Left to his own devices, he'd have chosen a tall, long-legged, busty model type. Someone he could dress up and show off, who'd cling to his arm and look at him adoringly and pretend not to have a brain in her head."

"It's not as if you aren't attractive."

She winced. Did he feel sorry for her? Why else would he be handing out compliments? "He called me 'troll.'" Saying the hated nickname out loud still hurt. "And he said I was too smart for my own good." Though at least she was smart enough not to feel insulted by his acknowledgment of her brains.

Patrick's knuckles on the steering wheel whitened. "You're not a troll," he said. "And I'd rather be with a smart woman than ten supermodels who play dumb."

"I don't guess you get many chances to guard supermodels," she said. "You might change your mind if you did."

She didn't give him a chance to hand out more false compliments. She sat forward and peered at the road ahead. "Are you sure we're headed the right way? This doesn't look like much of a road."

The graveled two-track had narrowed further, trees closing in on either side. They'd seen no sign of houses or other traffic in miles. "The map showed this as an alternate route." He glanced at the screen on the GPS unit mounted on the dash. "And the GPS shows we're headed in the right direction."

"It just doesn't look as if anyone has traveled this way in a while."

"That's good. Whoever is threatening you won't think to check this route."

"Maybe not." But her expression remained clouded.

They rounded a curve and he had to slam on the brakes to avoid hitting a tree. The huge pine lay across the road, branches filling their field of vision, the needles almost black against the white snow. Patrick shifted into Park and stared at the tree. It completely blocked both lanes.

"What do we do now?" Stacy asked.

He slipped his gun from his holster, making sure it was loaded and ready to fire, then grasped the door handle. "Stay here while I check things out," he said. "If anyone starts shooting, stay down."

Chapter Seven

The tree was positioned perfectly for an ambush, lying in the arc of a narrow, uphill curve with thick woods on either side. Keeping low and using the car as a shield, Patrick examined the snow around them for tracks, but found only the prints of squirrels and birds. He froze and strained his ears, listening, but heard only the pinging of the cooling engine and his own labored breathing.

Slowly, he made his way along the tree to the trunk, and felt some of the tension ease out of him when he saw the bare roots stretching toward the sky. This tree hadn't been cut, as he'd first suspected, but had fallen, toppling over in a storm, or from the weight of snow and age.

He holstered his weapon and balanced on the tree trunk to peer over the branches at the road beyond. The snow on that side looked much deeper, the route barely discernible. The tree had probably been here awhile. He jumped down and tramped back toward the car.

Stacy climbed out of the passenger side and met him halfway. "What were you looking at up ahead?" she asked. "What did you see?"

"Looks like the tree blew over in the last storm. The

road's completely blocked. We'll have to turn around and go back the way we came."

"Couldn't we move the tree or something?"

"Even if we could, the road up ahead hasn't been plowed. We'd never make it through."

"I can't believe we've wasted so much time coming all this way only to have to backtrack," she said.

"Me, too. But it can't be helped. And maybe doing so convinced the kidnappers that we've given up."

"How could anyone believe a mother would ever give up looking for her child?"

"Maybe they don't have children." He reached for the door handle as the glass in the door shattered into a thousand glittering shards.

"Get down!" he shouted, as he dived beneath the car. The sharp report of gunfire echoed through the canyon, the sound folding in on itself until the crescendo crackled like thunder. Bullets slammed into the side and top of the vehicle, rocking it from side to side and shattering the front windshield and mirrors.

"Stacy!" He turned his head, searching for her, but nothing moved in the limited area he was able to see from his place beneath the car. He slid sideways on his stomach, gravel digging into his elbows and knees. The silence following the gunfire pressed down on him, the only sounds the pinging of the cooling engine and the scrape of his body as he dragged it across the gravel.

He emerged on the opposite side of the car, using the vehicle as a shield between himself and the shooter. "Stacy?" he called again.

"Over here."

He followed her voice to a narrow space between two

boulders on the side of the road, but when he started toward her, another barrage of gunfire sent him diving for the cover of the vehicle.

"Patrick?" Her voice rose in alarm. "Are you all right?"

"I'm fine. Are you okay?"

"I'm okay. What are we going to do?"

He levered himself up just enough to peer over the hood of the car at the opposite side of the canyon. Nothing stirred in the red-and-gold rock cliffs, but the shots had definitely come from that direction. But where, exactly?

He slipped out of his coat, then searched the side of the road until he found a broken tree branch. He draped the coat over the branch and raised it up above the hood of the car. Shots erupted from an outcropping of rock opposite. Was it his imagination, or were these shots from a lower trajectory than the previous barrage? Was the gunman working his way down to them? Or was he simply moving in closer for a better chance to pick them off?

He glanced back over his shoulder toward the niche where Stacy sheltered. He couldn't see her, and he couldn't risk crossing the open space between her and the car. "Stacy, can you hear me?" he asked, keeping his voice low.

"Yes."

"I'm going to try to climb up and come in behind the shooter. But I need you to distract him while I get away."

"How can I do that?"

"I'm going to give you my gun and I want you to shoot up at the canyon wall—just enough to draw their fire. While they're focused on you, I'll get on the other side of the fallen tree and start up the canyon on the other side. I should be far enough down there that they won't be able to see me."

"I don't think we should split up," she said. "What if they do see you and shoot you?"

"I won't let that happen. If I don't try this, they'll just keep us pinned down here until dark, then they'll move in and pick us off."

Silence. Had he frightened her so much she was unable to speak?

"All right," she said after a long moment. "Tell me what to do."

"When I tell you, move as fast as you can to my side. Stay low."

"All right."

He sighted in on the rock outcropping and steadied his pistol on the hood of the car. "Now!" he called, and squeezed off three quick shots.

Stacy hurtled out of her hiding place and dived into the snow beside him as another hail of bullets shook the car.

Patrick helped her to sit up. Blood streaked her face. "You're hurt," he said.

She shook her head. "Just some broken glass that nicked my cheek. I'm fine. Now tell me what to do."

He fit a fresh magazine to the weapon and handed it to her. "See that rock outcropping up there—the one where there's a slash of almost purple-colored stone, sort of shaped like an arrowhead?"

She nodded. "I see it."

"When I give the word, start shooting at that outcropping. Just hold down the trigger and empty the magazine at that spot."

"You can't go up there without a gun."

"I have another." He slid the SIG Sauer from the ankle holster and checked the load. "I'm going to leave you with an extra magazine." He didn't explain she was to use the other bullets if their assailants slipped past him and came after her; she was smart enough to figure that out on her own.

She clutched the gun in both hands, keeping the barrel pointed at the ground. "Be careful," she said.

"I will." He rested his hand on her shoulder for a moment—she felt so small and fragile, yet she had more strength than some men he'd known. "Are you ready?"

She took a deep breath. "Yes."

He nodded and she took aim and began firing, splinters of rock exploding from the stone outcropping, the report of gunfire obliterating all other sound.

He ran, keeping low and moving in a zigzag pattern they'd drilled into him during training. The movement was supposed to make him a more difficult target to hit, but he doubted a spray of automatic weapons fire would miss. But his plan to focus the assailant's attention on Stacy seemed to have worked; he made it to the tree unharmed and dived over the trunk, landing in thick, soft snow on the other side.

Post holing through knee-deep drifts, he powered his way to the opposite bank and began making his way up the rocky slope. Ice, snow and loose rock made the climb difficult; for every foot he gained, he slid back six inches. The cold left his hands numb and penetrated his thin clothes until he shook from a bone-deep chill. Rocks tore at his clothing, cutting his skin, but he ignored the pain, pushing on.

When he judged himself to be a little above the outcropping where he'd spotted the shooter he began working his way sideways, scrambling over scrubby trees that clung to the side of the canyon, slipping in slush and loose gravel. Below, all was silent; even the echo of the gunfire had faded away.

His path intersected a narrow game trail, the hoofprints of deer clearly outlined in the snow along with the ridged soles of a man's hiking boots. Patrick examined the imprint; it was fresh and sharp, and similar prints led down the slope. The shooter had come this way to set up his post among the rocks.

He moved more slowly now, as soundlessly as possible, his pistol drawn and ready to fire. Soon he could look down into the niche formed by the outcropping of rock, a space just wide enough for a single man to crouch.

But the niche was empty. The snow around it was littered with spent bullet casings, the metal jackets glinting in the snow.

Patrick dropped into the niche and looked around. A search revealed an empty chip bag and sandwich wrapper, and the deep impression where someone had sat, possibly for a long time. Had someone staked out this area, just in case they'd decided to come this way? The idea that whoever was behind the kidnapping would have gone to such trouble—invested the manpower to cover even this remote route—disturbed him. Why was one little boy worth so much trouble and expense?

Whoever had been here wasn't here now. They'd

either anticipated his arrival and made their getaway while they had the chance—or they'd taken advantage of his absence to descend to the road, and Stacy. He'd heard no shots, but there were other ways of killing a person. The image of Stacy at the hotel, a knife to her throat, flashed through his mind, and a wave of sickness shook him.

"Stacy!" he shouted.

Stacy! echoed back to him from the canyon walls.

Half climbing, half sliding, he made his way down the side of the canyon. He tried to stay in cover, behind trees or boulders, but as he descended, no one shouted at him or fired at him or tried in any way to stop him. This indication that he was alone spurred him to move almost recklessly, stumbling down the steep embankment toward the car.

"Stacy!" he shouted again as he ran toward the vehicle. No answer came.

The car sagged in the roadway with three flat tires. Most of the windows were shattered, and bullet holes riddled the body. Patrick registered the damage as he made his way around the wreck, but there was no sign of Stacy. She wasn't underneath or inside, or back in the niche between the rocks where she'd initially sought shelter.

He examined the snow beside the car, but his own movements earlier had trampled it into slush. On his knees now, he studied the ground for the waffle-soled tread of the hiking boot he'd seen in the tracks on the opposite side of the canyon. He found a partial print that might have been a match, but he couldn't be sure. He started to stand, but a glint of something bright in the gravel caught his attention. He leaned forward and plucked a thin gold earring from the mud. His blood turned to ice as he recognized one of the hammered hoops Stacy had worn. She'd lost it here in the mud, in a struggle he hadn't been around to protect her from.

"No! LET ME GO!" Stacy tried to vent her rage on the man who held her in his unyielding grip, but he muffled her shouts with the sleeve of his jacket, shoving the fabric into her mouth until she was almost choking on the taste of dusty tweed. Thus silenced, she fought all the harder, kicking and scratching, but her struggles did nothing to slow his progress as he dragged her down the canyon. A second man trailed after them, an automatic weapon cradled in his arms as he scanned the embankments on either side of them.

Her heel connected hard with her captor's shin and he grunted and shifted his hold enough to uncover her mouth once more. "Let me go!" she screamed again.

The man with the gun was on her in two strides, punching her hard on the side of the face so that her vision blurred and her ears rang. "Shut up!" he commanded.

She blinked and his face returned to focus—a hard, lean face, skin stretched tight over wide cheekbones and a square jaw. His eyes were so pale they were almost colorless, like ice chips set in his face, and his expression was just as cold. It was a face she'd seen before, but the knowledge only confused her. This man had worked for Sam; she was sure of it. So why did he want to hurt her now?

He leaned close to speak to her, his breath smelling of stale coffee and cigarettes. "You make any more noise and I'll cut your tongue out." As if to demonstrate, he pulled a knife from his pocket and flicked open the blade.

She tried to swallow, but her mouth was dry. "What do you want with me?" she whispered.

His gaze swept over her, stripping her, reducing her to an object, not a person. "I want a lot of things," he said. "The question is, which do I want first?"

The man who was holding her laughed at this—an unpleasant, awful laugh without mirth.

The pale-eyed man touched the blade of the knife to her throat, to the soft space over her vocal cords. He made a flicking motion and she felt a stinging pain, then the trickle of blood against her skin. "Do you think you'll be more cooperative if I cut you first?" he asked.

She stared at him, terror rendering her speechless. "I think I'll have to cut you," he said. "For a start."

She stared into his eyes and saw her own death there—a slow, painful death. She had no idea why these men had taken her, but she knew she couldn't stay with them. She had to get away.

She closed her eyes and made herself go limp, pretending to faint. The bigger man who carried her laughed. "You scared her senseless," he crowed.

"She'll be easier to carry that way," the pale-eyed man said. "Hurry up. We're still a ways from the car."

"What about that marshal?" the big guy said.

"Someone will deal with him later. He won't get far with his car disabled."

The big man shifted her over his shoulder, carrying her with her head hanging down his back, one hand grasping her bottom obscenely. She kept her eyes shut and tried to review her options, but she didn't seem to have any. Except she believed she had to get away from them before they reached the car. Once inside a vehicle she would truly be at their mercy. They could knife her or shoot her or do whatever they wanted within the prison of a car. At least out here in the open she had a hope of outrunning them.

That was her first move, then. She had to find a way to make the big guy put her down before they reached the car. As soon as he lowered her to the ground, she'd take off running and take her chances. But what would make him want to put her down? She could be sick on him—except she'd never been able to throw up easily. Even when she was ill and emptying her stomach would have made her feel so much better, her body refused to vomit. Morning sickness for her had been constant nausea with little relief.

Being sick wasn't an option, so what did that leave?

It left her with no pride and no shame. In the battle between momentary embarrassment and saving her own life, she chose life. Taking a deep breath, she tensed her muscles. Here goes....

"What the hell!" The big man howled and loosened his hold on her.

"What is it?" the pale-eyed man said.

"She pissed on me!" The big man slung her to the ground. As soon as she was free of his grasp, she sprang to her feet and ran toward the cover of a copse of trees. The air around her exploded with gunfire. Bullets ricocheted off rocks and thudded into the dirt at her feet, but she refused to slow. Better to die in a hail of bullets than be cut to death by a knife.

She reached the trees and pushed into a deeper thicket, barbed vines cutting into her hands and face. She prayed she wouldn't be trapped in the underbrush, where Pale Eyes and his companion could easily pick her off. If she could push on through to more open ground she'd have a better chance of getting away, since the underbrush would slow the two big men even further.

What she would do then, she didn't know. Even if she could get back to the car, it wasn't drivable. Pale Eyes and his buddy had descended on her maybe fifteen minutes after Patrick had left her. Did this mean they'd met him on their way down and killed him? She had heard no shots, but Pale Eyes could have used his knife. She hoped somehow Patrick had survived, that he hadn't given his life in order to protect her.

Whatever had happened to him, though, she was on her own now. She was stranded in the wilderness, with no weapon, no transportation and not even a coat to keep her warm.

The idea that she might die of the cold after dodging bullets all afternoon brought tears to her eyes, but she pushed them away. She wasn't going to give up. Not when Carlo was waiting for her to come to him.

After what seemed like half an hour but was probably only a few minutes, she emerged into a clearing of tall grass and scattered boulders. She crouched behind one of the larger boulders, trying to catch her breath and listening for sounds of pursuit. But she heard nothing—no gunfire, no crashing through the underbrush, no running footsteps or shouts. Nothing but the rasp of her own breathing and the thud of her own heart.

"Stacy!"

Her name, shouted in the ringing silence, would have been startling enough, but the realization of who was calling for her made her jump up and push her way back through the underbrush toward the sound.

"Stacy!" Patrick shouted again. "It's all right. You can come out."

She emerged from the trees and stood on the side of the gravel road, looking back the way she'd come, at the two figures slumped in the gravel, at Patrick's feet. He held Pale Eyes's automatic weapon in one hand and his own pistol in the other. In the fading light she couldn't read the expression on his face, but the relief in his voice was clear as he called to her. "Stacy! Are you all right?"

"I'm okay." She began walking toward him. She was bleeding and wet and cold, and beginning to shake from the strain of it all. But she was alive, and Patrick hadn't given up on her. They were going to find Carlo. They were going to find her son, or die trying.

Chapter Eight

They found their attackers' car parked on the side of the road a quarter mile away, the keys in the ignition. A quick search of the backseat found ammunition for the weapons, some rope, a roll of duct tape and a couple blankets. The trunk contained two suitcases, an empty gas can and a spare tire. "Looks like they planned to tie you up and cover you with the blanket," Patrick said, tossing her one of the coverlets. "Wrap yourself up in this. You must be freezing."

"Maybe they were just going to wrap up my body until they could dispose of it," she said.

"It would have been easier to leave you for dead back on that deserted road." He slid into the driver's seat and cranked the engine. The deeper they got into this, the less sense it made. Kidnappers took the boy, but left Stacy unharmed. Then different men came back for Stacy. They hadn't killed her outright, which seemed to indicate they had intended to take her somewhere alive. The anonymous female caller threatened to kill Carlo if Stacy and Patrick kept coming after them, yet someone had set up an ambush on the most obvious secondary route for them to take. Once again, the attackers hadn't killed Stacy, but had seemed to want her alive.

When he'd come upon the two thugs they'd been firing into the underbrush, shouting for Stacy. He took up his position behind a rock and called to them and they turned their attention to him. He'd been close enough to pick them off before they killed him.

He turned the car around and set the heater to run full blast. By the time they reached the highway he was starting to feel his feet again.

Stacy stirred and rearranged the blanket more tightly around her. "I recognized one of those men back there," she said. "The tall one with the pale eyes. He worked for Sam."

He hadn't expected this; so far everyone they'd encountered had been a stranger to her. He slowed the car and glanced at her. "Are you sure?"

"Yes. I'd never forget a face like that." She pulled the blanket more tightly around her. "He creeped me out. He was always staring at me."

"What did he do for Sam? Do you know?"

"He was just another thug. Muscle. An enforcer."

"Was he at the house the day Sam was killed?"

"No. He didn't come to Colorado with us. He worked in New York. He wasn't one of the family bodyguards, or anyone who spent a lot of time around the house. He was just, you know, an employee. He came to the house a few times to meet with Sam."

"When was the last time you saw him?"

"A couple months ago?" She wrinkled her nose. "Maybe a little longer. Whenever he showed up I always left the room, so I have no idea why he was there."

"Who could he be working for now?"

"I have no idea about that, either."

"Do you remember his name?"

"No. I don't think I ever heard it. It's not like Sam introduced me to the people he worked with."

"My people will run his fingerprints—maybe they'll come up with a match. Did he say anything about why they wanted to kidnap you?"

Her face went a shade paler. "He said a lot of things about what he wanted to do to me—but nothing beyond threats. I thought he wanted to kill me, though I think he planned to…to hurt me first." She swallowed, visibly gaining control of her emotions.

He covered her hand with his own. "I don't think they—or whoever they were working for—wanted you dead. If that was the case, it would have been so much easier to leave your body in the canyon. Safer, too."

"But the caller said I was to stay away, and I thought since we hadn't, they wanted to punish me."

"We don't even know if the caller and these guys are connected. Or maybe the call was just a ploy to get us to take a different route. There aren't that many ways to get to Crested Butte. Whoever wants you could have reasoned it would be easier to stop us and separate us in a remote canyon. Did either of those men say anything to let you know what they were up to? Or who they worked for?"

"No. They never mentioned Carlo or where they were taking me or who they were working for or anything useful."

"What about the other guy? Did you recognize him?"

"Not really. But I didn't pay a lot of attention to the men who came and went at the house. I only remember the one guy with the pale eyes because he was so creepy."

Her voice shook, all the fear and terror of her ordeal condensed in those few words. "You did great," he said, hoping to bolster her spirits. "You kept your head and you didn't stop fighting. You got away."

"Thanks to you. I was afraid they'd found you first and killed you."

"They never saw me until it was too late."

"Well…I'm glad you're okay. I'm glad I'm not trying to find Carlo on my own."

She slumped against the car door, weariness in every inch of her posture. Fatigue dragged at him as well, the long hours and constant tension catching up with him. "You look exhausted," he said. "Even if we make it to Crested Butte, there's no way we can locate the ranch tonight. I think we should stop and rest before we go on."

"No, we have to keep going. If we can just get some coffee, I'll feel better."

"All right." Maybe coffee would help. And something to eat, though he wasn't hungry.

Over an hour passed before he spotted the gas station/convenience store set back from the highway. A sign advertised Beer and Bait and Clean Restrooms. "I'll fill up the car while we're here," he said, pulling up to the gas pumps. "This looks like the only place for miles."

"All right. I'll get some coffee and try to clean up a little in the ladies' room." She started to open the door, but he put a hand out to stop her.

"Here." He slipped out of his coat. "Your jacket's torn and muddy. Put this on."

"It's miles too big."

"Then it will cover more of you."

She looked down at her clothes, which were all but in tatters after her dash through the briars in the canyon. "I guess I am a mess. All right. Thanks."

She tossed the blanket in the backseat and pulled on his coat. She pushed the sleeves up and wrapped it around her as tightly as she could. She looked like a high school girl wearing her boyfriend's letter jacket. Cute.

"What are you smiling about?" she asked.

He hadn't even realized he'd been smiling. "Nothing. You go in and get what you want. I'll be there as soon as I'm done filling the tank."

When he came inside she was adding cream and sugar to a large cup of coffee. "You should get something to eat, too," he said.

"I'm not hungry."

"I know. But we'll both feel better if we eat."

She selected a couple granola bars while he added a ham sandwich to their purchases. While he waited for the clerk to tell him the total, he suppressed a yawn.

"I know the feeling," the clerk said. "I come on shift at three this morning—I was supposed to get off at eleven, but the other woman didn't come in, so I had to work a double."

"I'm going to go on outside to wait," Stacy said, gathering up her coffee and snacks.

"I'll be right out," he said. He handed a twenty to the clerk. "When you were working this morning, did you see a little boy, about three years old, with blond hair? He was probably with a man."

She counted out his change. "Who wants to know?"

He took out his ID. Showing it was a risk; if she'd

seen the bulletins saying Durango police were wanting
to question him, she might conclude he was a fraud or
somehow on the wrong side of the law and contact the
authorities. He didn't have time to waste straightening
out this mess. But if she had seen Carlo and his captors
it would confirm he was on the right track.

He decided to risk it, and flipped open the leather
folder. She studied it and nodded. "Who is it you're
looking for, again?"

He took out his phone and clicked on Carlo's picture.
"This is the boy I'm looking for. His name is Carlo. He
was taken from his mother last night. We think the men
who took him headed this way."

She leaned close to study the picture, then nodded.
"I saw him. At least I'm pretty sure it was him. He was
crying, kind of throwing a temper tantrum, the way kids
do when they're so tired. The man brought him in to go
to the bathroom and the boy didn't want to go back out
to the car. He sat down on the floor over there and the
man had to drag him away. All the while he was crying and calling for his mommy." She looked stricken.
"I wish I'd known. I thought he was just being a brat.
I always watch for those AMBER Alerts and such. I
haven't seen anything about this kid."

"It's a sensitive case. We're trying to keep it quiet for
now. Can you describe the man he was with?"

She frowned, concentrating. "He was maybe six feet,
kind of thin, dark clothes. He was bent over the boy, so
I never really saw his face."

Patrick slid the phone back into his pocket and
checked her name tag. "Thank you, Marne. You've

been very helpful. Did you see what kind of car they were in?"

She shook her head. "Sorry. They parked around on the side and it was dark over there."

"If you remember anything else, call this number. Let them know you spoke to me." He handed her his card.

"I will. I hope you find him."

"Thank you."

He waited until he'd driven away to tell Stacy. "We're on the right track," he said. "The clerk back at the store thinks she saw Carlo early this morning. He was with a man who sounds like the one who snatched him from your room."

"She did? Why didn't you tell me before?" She turned to look back the way they'd come. "We have to go back. I have to talk to her."

"There's no need for that. She already told me all she knew."

"Turn this car around now! I want to talk to her."

The intensity of her anger hit him like a wave. He held on to the steering wheel more tightly, half believing she'd rip it from his hands. "Will talking to her really make you feel better, or only upset you more?" he asked, trying to make his voice as calming and gentle as possible. "It would definitely upset you. Isn't it enough to know we're on the right track?"

She wilted back against the seat. "Nothing will be enough until he's safe again. But if I could just talk to her…." She looked back again, twisting her hands in her lap.

Common sense and all his training told him turning

around to talk to the clerk again would be a waste of time they could better use finding the uncle's ranch. But her longing to cling to even this tenuous contact with her son tore at him. He slowed the car, then pulled to the side of the road and headed back the way they'd come.

He pulled up to the front of the building and Stacy had unhooked her seat belt and opened the door before he'd even shut off the engine. He followed her into the store, where a pasty-faced young man looked up from behind the front counter. "Where's the woman who was working here a few minutes ago?" Stacy asked.

The man shook his head. "There's no woman working here," he said.

"Her name was Marne." Patrick approached the counter and showed the clerk his marshal's ID. "She was working a double shift. I spoke to her for several minutes."

"You must have the wrong store," the clerk said. "I don't know any Marne, and I'm the only one working today. I came on at seven this morning."

"You're lying." Stacy gripped the edge of the countertop and stood on tiptoe, leaning toward the taller young man. "We were just here and Marne was here. If this is your idea of a joke, it isn't funny."

"I swear, there's no one named Marne here. There's no one else here at all."

Patrick glanced at the camera mounted over the front camera. "You have security tapes. I want to see them."

"You'll have to talk to the manager about that. And he'll want a subpoena." The clerk raised his chin defiantly, but his gaze didn't meet the marshal's.

"Where's the manager?" Stacy asked. "I want to speak to him."

"He isn't here. He won't be in until tomorrow. But if you want to leave a name and number, I'll tell him to call you."

Patrick gently took Stacy's arm. "We're wasting our time here," he said. "Let's go."

"But he's lying! I know that woman was here. I saw her. You talked to her. Why is he lying?"

"Come on." Patrick urged her toward the door. "We'll figure this out, I promise."

Back in the car, he locked the doors, half-afraid Stacy would rush back into the store and physically attack the clerk. "He's lying," she repeated, sending a murderous look toward the clerk, who watched them with a sullen expression.

"Yes, he is." Patrick started the car and backed out of the parking space.

"Where are we going?" she asked. "Are you just going to let him get away with that? Maybe he's holding Marne hostage in a back room. Maybe she's in trouble because she talked to you."

"I think Marne is probably fine," he said. "Though her name likely isn't really Marne." He pulled out his phone and hit the speed dial button for his office.

"Who are you calling?" Stacy asked. "What are you going to do?"

"Give me Special Agent Sullivan." He pulled the car into a lay by about a mile from the store. "I'm going to get to the bottom of this," he said to Stacy. "Give me a little bit."

"Sullivan." The lieutenant's voice was brisk and confident.

"Thompson here. I need you to send a team out to Lakeside Grocery in Lakeside, Colorado, about two hours outside of Durango on Highway 50. Get a subpoena for the front counter surveillance tapes. I want to know the details and background on every clerk who worked there last night and today, and anyone who came in. I'm especially interested in an older female clerk with a name tag that says Marne, and a man who may have come in with the little boy we're looking for, Carlo Giardino. While you're at it, you should also get a team out to County Road 7N in the same area. We had a shootout with a couple guys who tried to kidnap Stacy."

"Any casualties?"

"Two."

Sullivan swore under his breath. "What is going on with this case?"

"That's what we're trying to find out. Focus on the gas station first—those guys in the canyon aren't going anywhere."

"Sure thing," Sullivan said. "What's up?"

"I talked to the clerk, Marne, a few minutes ago, and she told me she was working this morning when a man brought Carlo into the store to use the restroom. But when Stacy Giardino went back there to talk to her just now, there's a clerk—with no name tag—who swears there's no one named Marne there, and he's the only one on duty."

"You think someone set you up?"

"I do. See what you can find out and let me know."

"Where will you be?"

"We're headed to Crested Butte. I'm more and more convinced the boy is there."

"You could be headed into a trap," Sullivan said.

"It feels that way, but I'll be careful. Something big is going on here, and I want to know what."

"I'll get right on it."

He ended the call and slid the phone back into his pocket, then turned to Stacy. "You should have threatened that clerk," she said. "Made him tell you where Marne was."

"I'm sure that's what Sammy would have done."

She folded her arms across her chest. "It would have worked. The clerk would have talked."

"Maybe. Or someone watching in the back room would have opened fire and killed us all."

She pressed both palms to her forehead and moaned. "I don't understand what's happening," she said.

"I'm not sure," Patrick said. "But I think Marne was a plant. Someone told her to tell us about seeing Carlo and one of the kidnappers. Once she'd done her job, she was paid off and sent away."

"But why do that?"

"I don't know. Maybe to make sure we headed in the right direction. To lure us. All of this seems orchestrated to keep us eager to get to Crested Butte."

"But that doesn't make sense. Those men in the canyon tried to kill us. They must have been waiting to ambush us. And before that, we got the phone call warning us away."

"They tried to kill me. They wanted you alive. They tried to kidnap you. And maybe the warning was really to get me away—they still wanted you, but they needed to find a way to separate us."

"They threatened me. I think they wanted to take me away and torture you."

"Men like that think threats will make a captive more compliant and easier to handle. I'll admit, I'm impressed you got away from them."

"I'll do anything to save my son." She shifted in her seat and looked away.

"Since they couldn't kill me and they failed to bring you in, maybe plan B is to lure us to where they can try again."

"Are you saying the kidnappers want us to find them?"

"I think they want us where they can pick us off and shut us up," he said. "Whether or not Carlo is being held at his great-uncle's ranch, a remote property in a rural area sounds like an ideal place to get rid of the two people who have been interfering with the kidnappers' plans."

She pinched the bridge of her nose between her thumb and forefinger. "Are you saying the woman was lying, too—that she never saw Carlo?"

"I don't know. Maybe she saw him and maybe she didn't. Her job was to make us believe Carlo and the kidnapper passed through here so we'd keep following the trail of breadcrumbs."

"And are we going to keep following it?"

"I think we have to, but I want more information first."

"What kind of information?"

"I want to know who's behind this, for one thing."

"I thought we'd decided Uncle Abel was behind it. Isn't that why we're headed to Crested Butte?"

"But why would Abel want Carlo? He doesn't need him to step in and take control of the Giardino business. He's the only surviving Giardino male. He could just show up and start giving orders."

"I don't care why he's doing this—I just want my son."

"I want your son, too. But we can't go barging into an ambush. We need to know more about what we're dealing with."

"You're dealing with an old man who hasn't had anything to do with the family for years."

"But you said Sam threatened to turn the business over to him, passing over Sammy. That could mean the brothers had been in touch."

She shifted in her seat. "Maybe. Or maybe we're looking at this all wrong and Abel isn't the one behind this at all."

"If not Abel, who do you think it is?" he asked.

"I don't know. Maybe it's the old woman—his mother."

"You think Carlo's great-grandmother kidnapped him?"

"I think that woman is capable of anything." She shivered. "The one time I met her, she gave me the creeps. She was a regular witch, and she ordered everyone—including Sam—around like they were slaves."

"Maybe, but my instinct is that someone bigger is behind this." An eighteen-wheeler rocketed past on the highway, shaking the car.

"What do you mean, bigger?" Stacy asked.

"Think about it. Someone is going to a lot of trouble here—planting witnesses, tailing us. That takes manpower, and vehicles and weapons—all that adds up to a lot of money."

"Abel and his mother have money, I'm sure."

"Not that kind of money."

"So who do you think is behind this?"

"Do you remember I asked you about Senator Nordley?"

She nodded. "You think a senator masterminded all this? Why?"

"Power? Money? Because he has secrets he wants to stay secret?" Patrick shook his head. "I don't know, but word is that Nordley was behind Sam's escape from prison last year. And Anne—Elizabeth Giardino—said she saw him at the house right before our raid."

"But if Nordley was working with Sam, whatever secret he had died with Sam."

"Maybe. But maybe it's not about secrets. Maybe it's all about money. Politics is an expensive business. If an ambitious man like Nordley wanted to, say, run for president, he'd need a great deal of money to do so. The Giardinos have that kind of money. If he did a favor for the family, they would want to reward him."

She considered this. He was glad now he'd brought up the subject. He'd been a little worried she'd become hysterical, or more distraught, but he should have known better. She was sharp, and talking with her was helping him to organize his own thoughts and theories. She'd said she wanted to be a lawyer, but she would have made a good agent, too.

"So you think Nordley helped kidnap Carlo for Uncle Abel? But why? It still doesn't make sense."

"No, it's doesn't," he admitted. "But I'm going to keep working at it until it does make sense. After that, we'll know the best move to make." He put the car into gear.

"Where are we going?" she asked.

"We need to find a place to hole up for a while, to plan our next move."

"No!" The fierceness of her objection—the sudden change from calm to agitated—unsettled him. Yes, she'd been through a lot, and her emotions were on edge, but she'd never struck him as the hysterical type. He hesitated, his hand on the gearshift.

"The more we delay, the more danger Carlo may be in," she said. "We have to go to him now."

"We don't even know for sure he's at the ranch—or where the ranch is, exactly," he said. "We'll be putting him in greater danger if we barge in without a plan. And we'll be putting ourselves at risk, too." He turned his attention back to the road and prepared to pull the car out onto the highway.

"Stop!"

He groaned. This was not an argument he wanted to have. What had happened to the reasonable woman he'd been admiring only seconds before? "Look, Stacy—" He turned to her and the words died on his lips.

She held a gun in both hands and it was aimed right at him. "I won't let you keep me from my son," she said.

Chapter Nine

Patrick had faced down his share of desperate men and women with guns, but the sight of Stacy holding a weapon on him made his blood run cold. Her hands shook so badly she could scarcely keep the weapon still. He wasn't so worried that she'd deliberately shoot him, but that the gun would accidentally go off. At this close range she'd be unlikely to miss. "Stacy, put the gun down," he said, his words soft, each one carefully enunciated.

"No. Not until we're in Crested Butte. Drive."

"We're still hours away. Are you going to hold the gun on me the whole way?"

"If I have to." Her gaze met his, defiant—but he glimpsed the fear behind her bravado.

"Stacy, I don't believe you really want to kill me. I'm on your side, remember?"

"You say that, but why won't you take me to where you know Carlo is?" Her lip trembled. "Why are you keeping me from my son?"

"We don't know where he is. We still have to find the ranch and then we need to determine he's there. We can't just go barging in. He might be hurt. I know you don't want that."

"I just want my boy!" The words ended on a wail and the barrel of the gun dipped lower. Great. Now if she fired she'd blast him right in the crotch.

He shifted in his seat. "I want to find your son," he said. "I want to see the two of you safely together. But I won't do anything to jeopardize his life. Or yours."

"At least in Crested Butte we'd be closer. We could find him. I might see him on the street."

"Crested Butte is still two hours away, at least. We're both exhausted. We're dirty and cold and you're hurt."

"I'm fine."

"You've got cuts and scratches and bruises all over your face and hands. Your clothes are filthy and neither of us has had six hours of sleep in the past forty-eight. If we're going to help Carlo, we need to be strong and rested and sharp."

She looked away, the gun dipping farther. He kept his eyes on her, waiting. "When will I see him again?" she asked.

"Maybe as soon as tomorrow. It depends on what we learn."

"Then why can't we go to Crested Butte and look for him now?"

"That's what the people we're dealing with seem to want us to do. I think we'd be safer if we stopped somewhere more out of the way. We can rest and come up with a plan—one that will keep Carlo safe and alive."

She brought the gun up once more. "I just want this to be over," she said softly.

"So do I. But shooting me won't bring back your son. I really do want to help, if you'll trust me."

She wet her lips. "I haven't had a lot of people in my

life I could trust. You're a lawman. Why should you be any different?"

From what she'd told him, every man she'd ever known, from her father to her husband, had betrayed her. He wouldn't add his name to the list. "You can trust me because I haven't let you down so far. Have I lied to you or done anything to hurt you?"

She bit her lip, then shook her head.

He held out his hand. "Will you give me the gun?"

She hesitated, then nodded and let him take the weapon from her hand. Only when he held the gun did the tension drain from his shoulders. Exhaustion buffeted him and he had to fight to tuck the gun safely under the seat and put the car in gear. "Are you okay?" he asked.

"Yes." She closed her eyes and swayed a little in her seat. She was so pale, the scratches and bruises on her face standing out against her ivory skin. "As all right as I can be."

Twenty minutes later, he turned in at a blue neon sign that advertised Motel. The old-fashioned tourist court was a low-slung row of rooms with doors painted bright turquoise, opening onto a gravel lot. Patrick paid cash for a room to an older man who wore suspenders and a checked shirt. No more flashing his credentials unless it was absolutely necessary. He and Stacy needed to fly under the radar now.

"You want ice, it's a quarter," the man said.

Patrick fished a quarter from his pocket and slid it across the counter. The old man shuffled off to a back room and returned shortly with a plastic bucket of ice. He handed it over while frowning at Stacy, who'd insisted on coming inside. "You sure you're okay, miss?" he asked.

She gave him a wan smile. "I'm just tired."

"You look like somebody beat you up." The clerk scowled at Patrick.

"I was in a car wreck," Stacy said. She took Patrick's arm and leaned against him. "I'll be fine. My husband is taking good care of me."

He was aware of her warm body pressed against his all the way back to the car. He parked in front of the room and carried both suitcases and the weapons inside, wrapping the guns in the blankets to hide them from anyone who might be watching. "Why did you tell the clerk I was your husband?" he asked.

"I thought he'd be less suspicious if he thought we were married. He was looking at you like he wanted to call the police. I had to do something."

"A car wreck was quick thinking."

"I'm sorry about before," she said. "When I pulled the gun on you. I wasn't thinking. I—"

"It's all right. You've been through a lot. Come here and sit down." He motioned toward the bed.

She looked wary. "Why?"

"I want to take a look at those cuts. I found a first aid kit in the trunk."

She sat on the edge of the bed and he angled the lamp shade to give him a better view of her uptilted face. The gash on her forehead where Carlo's kidnapper had hit her had scabbed over, and the bruising around it was an ugly purple and yellow, the skin slightly puffy and raised. He cleaned it with a cotton ball dipped in antiseptic, then dabbed antibiotic ointment along it, before covering it with a gauze pad held in place with strips of surgical tape. "I should have done this before now," he said.

"We haven't exactly had a lot of free time," she said.

He began cleaning the dozens of other scratches on her cheeks and along her jaw. "You look like you ran through a rosebush," he said, pausing to pluck a thorn from alongside her ear.

"I didn't stop to identify the local flora. Maybe they were wild roses."

He dabbed ointment on the deepest of the scratches, then cradled her jaw in his hand and turned her head to study the bruise along the side of her face. "Which one of those thugs did this?" he asked.

She closed her eyes and swallowed. "The one with the pale eyes. He threatened to cut out my tongue."

He forced himself to relax his hold on her jaw, to continue tending to her wounds without comment. He was getting good at holding back his anger, but he couldn't hold back his memories of another hotel room and another woman whose cuts and bruises he'd nursed like this. His sister was safe and well now, long free of her abuser, but the years when she'd suffered and he'd been unable to help her had left their scars.

"Do they make you take first aid when you train to be a marshal?" she asked.

"I was a Boy Scout." He leaned back to study his handiwork. She was still a mess, but with luck none of her injuries would become infected, and she'd heal without any major scars.

"Let me guess—you were an Eagle Scout."

"Yes."

She looked triumphant. "I knew it. Eagle Scout to U.S. Marshal. I guess it makes sense."

"There was a stint in Iraq in between. College before that."

"Did you think when you were doing all that you'd end up babysitting a mafia wife?"

"It's a little more than that, don't you think?" Her eyes met his and he felt the jolt of connection, and the weight of emotions he didn't dare examine too closely.

He stepped back, and began packing up the first aid kit. "Why don't you take a shower? I'll see what I can find for dinner. I think we passed a café right before I turned in here."

He felt her gaze on him for a long moment before she stood and went into the bathroom. Only when he heard the door close behind her did he raise his head to stare after her. He was treading on shaky ground here. In his career with the U.S. Marshal's office, he'd shepherded half a dozen women through the Witness Security program, many of them single, beautiful and vulnerable. He'd never crossed the line that separated professional from personal. But Stacy had him tiptoeing across that line, contemplating how close he could get before he reached a point where he could never go back.

A SHOWER REVIVED Stacy somewhat. Afterward, she stood wrapped in a towel, contemplating her ruined clothing. Between the mud, brambles, blood and other bodily fluids to which the garments had been subjected, they were little better than rags, but, since she had nothing else to wear, she had no choice but to wash them. She dumped the rest of the bottle of hotel shampoo in the tub and added several inches of hot water, then dumped the clothing in to soak.

Patrick was gone—she assumed to get dinner—when she emerged from the bathroom. She spied the suitcases by the door and hefted one onto the bed. The two thugs were unlikely to have anything that would fit her, but even a T-shirt and boxers would do for sleeping. Fortunately, Pale Eyes or his buddy hadn't bothered to lock the bag. She unzipped it and breathed a sigh of relief when she spotted clean boxers and socks. No T-shirts, but she found a man's dress shirt, neatly folded and still in a bag from the cleaners.

By the time Patrick returned with two plastic bags, she'd changed into the borrowed clothing and sat cross-legged on the bed, rifling through the rest of the contents of the suitcase. The marshal paused in the doorway. "Feeling better?" he asked.

"Much. I'm washing my clothes, so I borrowed some from our two late friends. There's probably stuff in here that will fit you."

"Good idea." He set the bags on the table by the window. "Anything else interesting?"

"One of them liked science-fiction novels." She tossed a paperback onto the bed. "And one of them wore a night guard." She pointed to a case for the dental appliance. "Who knew?"

"What about the other case?" he asked.

"I haven't checked it yet."

"We'll take a look after we eat. I got a couple burgers. There wasn't much choice."

"I'm so hungry, I could eat almost anything."

She followed him to the table, where he unpacked

the food from one of the plastic bags. "What's in the other bag?" she asked.

"Since we had to leave everything back at the other car, I picked up a few things—toothbrush, toothpaste, a razor, things like that."

She peered into the bag, then reached in and pulled out a tube of lipstick and a powder compact. The lipstick was pink. "I'm guessing these aren't for you."

The tips of his ears turned almost as pink as the lipstick, though his face remained impassive. She suppressed the urge to giggle. There was something about an otherwise tough guy who got embarrassed about buying a girl makeup that was sweet—as was the purchase in the first place. "I notice you went to a lot of trouble to fix yourself up before," he said. "I thought it might help you feel better."

"You thought right. Thank you." She resisted the urge to kiss his cheek—just as a gesture of thanks. That might be taking things too far.

They sat across from each other at the little table, eating burgers and fries and drinking from bottles of water. The food tasted good, but as her hunger abated, the familiar anxiety about the future returned. "What do we do next?" she asked.

"In the morning I'll call my office again—see if they've come up with an address for Uncle Abel." He wiped mustard from the corner of his mouth with a paper napkin. "I also want to know if they've found out any more about Sam and Sammy's wills."

"So you still believe Carlo's kidnapping is related to the will?"

"People commit crimes for many different reasons,

but a lot of times they're motivated by what they stand to gain, such as money, power or revenge. A three-year-old doesn't have any power. Kidnapping him hurts you the most. Have you thought of anyone who would use Carlo to get back at you?"

She shook her head. "The only person who hated me that much is dead."

"Are you talking about Sammy?"

Yes, Sammy. Her not-so-dear departed spouse. "Don't tell me a husband can't hate his wife, because he can."

"Did you feel the same way about him?"

"Sometimes I thought I did…." She studied the remains of her hamburger, her appetite fading. "Other times… In the beginning, things between us were pretty good. Sammy was sweet on our honeymoon. He seemed to really like me, and we had fun. But later, after Carlo was born…" She shook her head. Nothing she'd done had pleased her husband, and he'd lost the desire to please her. After a while it felt safer to stop trying.

"Did he hit you?" Patrick's voice was low, his gaze boring into her, as if the answer to this question made a difference to him.

"No. He was proud of that. 'You can't say I'm cruel,' he used to tell me. 'I never hit you.' But there are worse things than being hit. Bruises and even broken bones can heal, but the things people say to you… Those wounds can go a lot deeper." She felt the pain from those injuries still—maybe some of them would never heal.

She waited for him to ask what Sammy had said to her, but he didn't. Maybe he respected her privacy too much—or maybe he didn't really care. Why should he? Though he'd seemed concerned about her welfare, maybe that was just part of doing his job. Mr. Eagle Scout would never shirk his duty.

She set aside the remains of her burger. "Why don't we see what's in the other suitcase?" she said. "Maybe there's some clothes you can wear."

He looked down at his mud-stained shirt and jeans. "You think I need new clothes?"

"I think it's a miracle the motel clerk didn't call the police. You look like a derelict."

He rubbed his hand over his chin, and the scrape of bristles against his palm sent a hot shiver up her spine. "I could probably do with a little sprucing up." He leaned over and grasped the handle of the second suitcase. "Let's see what my options are."

He tugged, but the case didn't budge. "I remember this one was heavy," he said. He stood and used both hands to heave the suitcase onto the bed.

Stacy stood beside him as he unzipped the top and folded it back. She let out a squeak, and covered her mouth with her closed fist. "Is that real?" she asked, her voice scarcely above a whisper.

Patrick nodded, and reached into the case and took out a stack of bills from the rows and rows of similar stacks filling the case. "It looks real to me," he said. "There must be thousands of dollars in here. But what were our two late friends doing with it?"

Chapter Ten

Stacy stared at the suitcase full of money. It didn't even look real, so much of it all together. "How much do you think is in there?" she asked.

Patrick rifled through the stacks of bills. "Looks like all twenties, in bundles of fifty—I'd guess fifty thousand dollars."

She sank onto the bed. "What were those two doing with that much money?"

He felt along the side of the case and in all the pockets. "There's nothing else in here—no notes or ID or anything like that."

"It's the kind of thing you see in those TV mysteries," she said. "The unmarked bag of bills, dropped off in the park to pay ransom. But ransom for whom? Have they kidnapped someone besides Carlo?"

Patrick pulled out his phone. "Let's see if headquarters knows anything."

While he waited on hold to speak to who knows who, Stacy looked through the other suitcase—the one with the clothes. She found another science-fiction novel, a phone charger (but no phone) and an open box of condoms. Nothing incriminating or even threatening. Except for the fact that they'd attacked her and Patrick with guns and knives, they might have been any traveling businessmen.

"Let me know what you find. I'll call back in the morning." Patrick ended his call and slid his phone back into his pocket. "They're going to do a trace for large sums of missing cash, but I'm not holding out much hope that that will turn up anything. A team is on its way to the canyon to see if they can ID the guys."

She studied the open suitcase. "Maybe we could trade the cash for Carlo."

"We could try—if we knew how to get in touch with whoever has him." He closed the suitcase and set it on the floor. "I'm going to take a shower. You should try to get some sleep. Maybe we'll be able to get more information in the morning."

He took some clothes from the other suitcase and carried them and the plastic bag of toiletries into the bathroom. In a few minutes, she heard the shower running.

Stacy lay back on the bed, on top of the covers. One bed. That was all right. Sleeping with Patrick last night had been nice—even if they were only sleeping. She'd never met a man like him. He could be hard, brutal even—he hadn't hesitated to kill three men to save their lives. But he'd been so gentle, too, when he was tending her wounds, or when he held her while she cried.

He was the kind of man she wished Sammy had been. But Sammy had never looked at her the way Patrick did—as if she was an intelligent person whose opinions mattered. As if she *counted.*

And she could never think of Sammy the way she thought of Patrick—that he was a good man who deserved her respect and admiration. All the bad things Sammy had done had blotted out any good that might have remained, whereas the more she knew about Patrick, the more good there was to see.

She closed her eyes, the soothing rhythm of the water in the shower beating against the tile lulling her to sleep. She dreamed she was on a beach with Patrick, and they were lying in the warm sun and he was smiling and taking her in his arms....

PATRICK LIFTED STACY and held her close, her head resting against his chest, his heartbeat a steady, strong rhythm in her ear. His hands caressed her back, and she slid her arms around his neck and snuggled closer, pressing her breasts against his bare chest, her nipples straining against the thin fabric of the T-shirt.

He grew still, his heart beating harder in her ear. "I didn't mean to wake you," he said softly. "I was just trying to get you under the covers."

She opened her eyes, the fog of sleep clearing as she stared up at him, at the jut of his chin and the masculine plane of his freshly shaved cheek in profile. He smelled of soap and shaving cream and warm male skin. This wasn't a dream or a fantasy; he was really holding her in his arms. And the thought of him releasing her and moving away, as much as the memory of her erotic dreams, made her brazen.

"I'll get under the covers if you'll get under there with me," she said. She smoothed her palm down the taut muscles of his chest to his flat abdomen, stopping just short of the waistband of his boxers.

He took her by the upper arms and gently pushed

her away from him. "I'd better sleep on the floor to-night," he said.

She looked into his eyes, feeling bolder than she had in a long time. Maybe because she'd reached the point where she had nothing to lose. She'd given up everything—her name, her dignity, even her child. She had nothing left but the need to be honest with herself about what she really wanted, and right now, she wanted Patrick. "Don't sleep on the floor," she said. "I want you to sleep with me. To make love with me."

"I don't think that would be a good idea." He rubbed his hands up and down her arms, a gentle caress that negated his words.

"Because you think it would be unprofessional?" She trailed her hand along his jaw, enjoying the smooth coolness of the freshly shaved skin.

"I'm supposed to be protecting you," he said.

"No one's going to hurt me while you're this close." She kissed him just below the ear, then began feathering kisses along the path her hand had just traced.

"Stacy, no." He cradled the side of her head.

"Don't tell me you haven't felt this…this heat be-tween us," she said. She held her breath, waiting for him to lie.

"I've felt it," he said, his voice rough with emotion.

She leaned back to look up at him. She wanted to see his face, to read all the emotion there. "We've been through hell the past couple days," she said. "I can't think of much worse. I've been terrified and hurt and my whole life right now feels like a nightmare. I can't think about the future and I don't want to relive the past. All I can do is hang on to this moment and focus on getting through the next day, the next hour, the next minute."

"You should sleep," he said. "We both should sleep."

"Or we could lie down together on this bed and forget about everything else for a while by focusing on each other. We could give in to that attraction we've both felt and create at least one good memory from this whole mess."

"I am attracted to you." He smoothed his hand down her shoulder, his thumb grazing the side of her breast and sending a tremor through her. "But duty doesn't always allow me to do the things I want."

Heaven save her from logical, steadfast men. She'd heard that men liked women who played hard to get, but apparently the reverse was true—the more Patrick resisted, the more she wanted him, and the more she was determined to persuade him. "You'll be right here with me. You said yourself we can't do anything else until the morning. We're stuck here in this room. In this bed." She took his hand and kissed his palm. "Please. I don't want to beg, but I need you tonight. And I think you need me."

"What about protection?"

She laughed. Even on the verge of giving in, he was still so calm and practical. "There's a box of condoms in the suitcase. More than enough, trust me."

"Then I guess we have everything we need." His eyes met hers, the intensity of his gaze pinning her back against the pillows and stealing her breath. "If you're sure this is what you want," he said. "Because once this starts between us, I don't know if I can stop."

He would stop if she asked; he was that kind of man.

But she wouldn't ask. "I want this, Patrick," she said. "I want you."

He leaned forward, covering her with his body, lips pressed to hers, chest flattening her breasts, stomach to stomach and thigh to thigh. He held himself up just enough to keep from crushing her, but the weight of him felt good. She wanted him close—even closer. She shifted to shape herself more firmly to him and opened her mouth to deepen the kiss. His tongue caressed and claimed her, and she reveled in the sensation.

He was such a contradiction—hard muscle and tender caresses, insistent pressure and whispered encouragement. He helped her out of the boxers, and then the shirt, so that she lay alongside him naked. She should have felt vulnerable—exposed. But seeing her reflection in his eyes, she felt more beautiful than ever.

He shaped his hand to her breast and dragged his thumb over the distended nipple, eliciting a gasp. "You're really special, did you know that?" Then, not waiting for an answer, he bent his head and covered her breast with his mouth.

She closed her eyes and surrendered to the heat and light he sent coursing through her. Waves of feeling she'd almost forgotten could exist washed over her. He turned his attention to her other breast, then moved lower, trailing kisses along her ribs and across her abdomen.

She arched to him and felt him smile against the curve of her thigh and press her down into the mattress. "Don't be impatient," he said.

"I feel as if we've waited so long," she said.

"We can wait a little longer. It will be worth it." As

if to prove his point, he ran his tongue along the sensitive folds of her sex. She bit back a moan and felt him smile again. He was normally so solemn; she liked the idea that she could make him smile this way.

ONE OF PATRICK'S former supervisors had labeled him single-minded—so intently focused on one task he failed to notice anything else. The man hadn't meant it as a compliment, but Patrick saw this talent for intense concentration as a gift sometimes.

At this moment, he wanted nothing more than to focus all his senses on the woman in his arms—on the silken feel of the skin of her thighs, on the intoxicating scent of her, on her sweet taste on his tongue. For these few minutes or hours he could lose himself in her, devote his full attention to pleasuring her and receiving pleasure in return.

She sighed and shifted beneath him, arching to him, a sweet offering and a silent plea. He rested his hand on her stomach, a gentling gesture. He was so tempted to bring her to release right away, but that would be cheating them both. Instead, he left her wanting, and moved away from her.

"Where are you going?" she asked.

He smiled and removed his boxers, his erection straining toward her. If she'd had any doubts about how much he wanted her, surely that would be erased now. He dug in the suitcase until he found the box of condoms. Whatever else the two thugs who attacked them had been up to, at least one of them had planned on getting lucky.

She sat up and reached out her hand. "Let me," she said.

"I don't think that would be a good idea." Even her gaze on him was enough to make him lose focus; at her touch he might go off like a rocket, spoiling this for them both.

He carefully rolled on the condom, then knelt on the bed beside her. "You're so beautiful," he said, caressing her breast. She was so petite and perfectly proportioned.

"Flattery will get you everywhere. Now come here, handsome." She reached for him and he moved between her legs. He didn't ask if she was sure or if she was ready; the answers to those questions were clear in her actions.

He was a man who lived his life by control. His survival and the survival of those he was assigned to protect relied on his vigilance. He had to always be on guard, aware, in charge. But with Stacy he was able to surrender, to lose himself in passion and pleasure.

She responded with similar abandon, opening to him fully, then wrapping her legs around him to keep him close, meeting him thrust for thrust. And all the while she looked into his eyes, holding him with her gaze, letting him see all her emotions—an offering as intimate and intense as the giving of her body.

He waited for her, feeling the tension within her build, doing whatever he could to coax her to her release. When at last she came with a loud cry he followed her quickly over the edge, holding her close, rocking together with her, moving as one, unable to tell where his pounding heart ended and hers began.

When at last he withdrew to lie beside her, she shocked him by bursting into sobs.

"Stacy, what is it?" He bent over her, alarmed. "Did I hurt you? What's wrong?"

"I'm sorry. I didn't mean…" She shook her head and tried to push him away. "I'm just being stupid, I—"

"You're not stupid." He pulled several tissues from the box by the bed and handed them to her. "What's happened to upset you?" he asked. "I really want to know."

"It wasn't you, I promise." She blew her nose. "I'm such a mess."

Maybe this was grief over her husband, finally hitting her. Or a memory of something else—the human mind was a funny thing, and emotions could sneak up on people. "Maybe it would help to talk about it," he said.

She nodded and dabbed at her eyes with a fresh tissue, then looked up at him through a fringe of lashes glittering with tears. "Being with you, just now, was so wonderful. I was afraid no man would ever want to touch me like that again." Her voice broke on a fresh sob.

He caressed her cheek. "It was wonderful for me, too. I've wanted you from that first night at the hotel."

She turned away from his touch, her shoulders hunched, and refused to look at him. "My husband— Sammy—hadn't touched me for at least two years. He told me no man would want a woman like me, that that was why my father had to sell me to the Giardinos, because he knew no other man would want me."

"If he wasn't already dead I'd make him wish he

was." Patrick closed his eyes against a surge of anger, the rage a physical thing that heated his blood and shook him. "He was lying. And he was a fool." He took a deep breath, struggling for calm. Sammy was gone now; there was nothing Patrick could do to hurt him. He needed to focus on Stacy. He gathered her close and kissed her—he kissed the top of her head and the side of her face and the tip of her nose before lingering at her lips, trying to tell her without words how worthy she was of all the love her monster of a husband had denied her.

She began crying again, the tears flowing silently down her cheeks. He tasted them, salty and sweet, the taste of his own mixed emotions of regret and longing.

He pulled her down beside him and held her, the covers pulled up over them, her head cradled against his chest, until her tears were spent, and she sighed again. "I'm sorry," she said. "That's not the reaction a man wants after making love to a woman."

"I'd rather you be honest with me than pretend," he said.

"That's one of the things I like about you. You don't lie, even when lying would be more convenient."

"You've had enough of lies. Including all the ones Sammy told you. Don't believe him."

"I try. But sometimes it's hard."

He squeezed her shoulder. "Maybe when this is all over it would be a good idea for you to talk to someone. A counselor. I could give you a name."

"Yeah. That probably would be a good idea." She snuggled down more tightly against him. "Thank you, for everything."

"Try to get some sleep," he said. "We've got a big day tomorrow."

"Maybe I'll get to see Carlo."

"Maybe you will." And maybe he'd figure out a way to say goodbye that wouldn't end up hurting them both.

POUNDING ON THE door woke them. The room was pitch-black and Patrick groped for his phone on the bedside table. The display showed 5:00 a.m.

"Who is it?" Stacy sat up beside him, the covers clutched to her chin.

Patrick reached for his pants as the pounding repeated. "Open up!" a deep voice demanded. "This is the police."

Chapter Eleven

Stacy stared at the door, heart pounding. Could she possible have heard them right? "What are the police doing here?" she whispered to Patrick.

"I don't know." He zipped his pants and pulled on a shirt. "Hold on. I'm coming!" he called.

"I'd better get dressed, too," Stacy said. She looked around for the shirt she'd discarded last night, but realized Patrick was wearing it.

"Better stay put," he said, as the pounding rattled the door frame again.

"Open up or we're coming in!"

Patrick jerked open the door and a beefy uniformed officer all but fell inside. Patrick stepped back, keeping his hands in clear view. "Can I help you?" he asked.

A second, older officer followed the first one inside. "Are you driving the black sedan parked in front of this room?" he asked.

"Is something wrong with the car?" Patrick asked.

The older cop's eyes narrowed. "I need to see some ID, Mr...."

"United States Marshal Patrick Thompson." He handed over his credentials.

The officer's eyebrows rose as he studied the ID. He glanced at Stacy. "And this woman is?"

"A material witness in a federal case."

The officer took in the single bed, clothes scattered around it. "Riiight," he said, drawing out the word.

Stacy felt her face heat, then bristled. She'd done nothing to be ashamed of—the police were the ones who ought to be ashamed, barging in on them this way.

"We're going to need the two of you to come with us down to the station for questioning about the murder of two men on County Road 7N yesterday afternoon," the older officer said. He returned Patrick's ID to him.

"I killed those men," Patrick said. "They ambushed us in the canyon and attempted to kidnap this woman."

The younger officer spoke up for the first time. "Why didn't you report this to our office?"

"This is a federal case. I reported it to my office and they're sending investigators. How did you find out about it?" Patrick's face was impassive, but Stacy felt the temperature in the room drop a few degrees at his chilly tone.

"A couple out snowshoeing stumbled on the bodies," the older officer said. "Then the hotel owner called to report a couple suspicious customers." He glanced at Stacy again. She pulled the covers more tightly around her neck—not because she was ashamed, but because the draft from the open door was freezing.

The officer turned back to Patrick. "If you'll both get dressed and come with us, I'm sure we can get this all sorted out."

"I'm sure that won't be necessary," said a commanding voice from behind the officers.

The police moved aside to reveal a slender man in a dark suit and overcoat. He flashed an ID badge. "Special Investigator Tim Sullivan," he said. He nodded to Patrick, then to Stacy, as if he found naked women in the beds of his coworkers every day of the week.

"Agent Sullivan…" the older officer began.

"Thank you for your help, officers," Sullivan said. "We can handle things from here. We promise to send your office a full report of our investigation."

"The crime occurred in our jurisdiction," the younger officer protested. "I believe—"

"I believe you don't want to be charged with interfering with a federal case."

Agent Sullivan's tone, as much as his words, made the officer blanch. He turned to his companion. "We'll be going now."

"Good."

When the door had closed behind the two officers, Agent Sullivan turned and regarded Patrick and Stacy. "I think, Marshal Thompson, you might have a little explaining to do."

"And I think you two should continue your discussion outside," Stacy said, "so that I can get dressed."

Sullivan tilted his head, as if considering the question. Stacy was sure he was about to make an off-color remark, but the glower on Patrick's face apparently made him think better of it. "Of course," he said. He glanced at Patrick's bare feet and unbuttoned shirt. "I'll meet you outside."

Patrick retrieved his shoes, then fished a clean pair of socks from the suitcase and sat on the side of the bed to put them on. Stacy studied his back, trying to read his thoughts in the tension there. "What happens now?" she asked.

"Maybe he's learned something about the where-abouts of the ranch, or Carlo." He drew up one leg and began tying the laces of his shoe.

"They won't pull you off the case, will they?"

He stilled. "Maybe they should."

"No!" She leaned forward and rested one hand on his shoulder.

"I've broken pretty much every rule and behaved unprofessionally. They'd be justified in pulling me off the case."

"I won't let them," she said. "Not when we've come so far. You know me and you know the case. I trust you."

He turned his head to meet her gaze at last. "We've crossed the line. You're not just a stranger I'm duty bound to protect."

"Does that mean you'll be any less committed to keeping me safe or helping me?"

"It means I've lost my objectivity. That could affect my judgment."

"I won't let them take you away from me. I won't."

He turned his back to her again and finished tying his shoe. "That could be up to Sullivan." He straightened. "You'd better get dressed." He walked out the door, not looking at her again.

SULLIVAN STOOD IN the light from a single bulb that il-luminated the stairwell several doors down from the room. Patrick moved toward him, zipping up his coat as he did so.

"You look like someone dragged you through the mud." Sullivan nodded at a smear of dirt on the sleeve of the jacket.

"Those two in the canyon ambushed us. I thought I'd sneak up behind them and they moved in and tried to kidnap Stacy."

"And you shot them."

"Yes."

"How gallant."

"I was doing my job. You would have done the same."

"Maybe."

"How did you end up here?" Patrick asked. "Your timing is uncanny, by the way. The local cops were ready to haul us off to jail."

"We had someone monitoring the scanner. They heard the call go out."

"You must have been close."

"We were at that convenience store. Nobody knows anything about anyone named Marne."

"What about the surveillance tapes?"

"What do you know—the machine had a malfunction and stopped working for half the day yesterday."

Patrick grunted and shoved both hands in his coat pockets. Neither man spoke for a long moment. An eighteen-wheeler sped by on the highway, Jake brakes rattling as it headed down the grade.

"Want to tell me what's going on with you and the Giardino woman?" Sullivan asked.

"No." He blew out a breath. "I know I screwed up. It just…happened."

"Sometimes it does. Is it going to affect your ability to do your job?"

"No." He faced the other man, surprised at the sympathy he found there. "I'm not some besotted schoolboy. I know how to handle myself."

"What about her?" He tipped his head toward the hotel room. "Women sometimes read more into these things."

"Stacy's concerned for her son. She knows what happened between us.... She knows there's no future there."

"Does she?"

"She's a lot stronger than she looks. Stronger than anyone I've known. Are you going to report us?"

"I don't work for the U.S. Marshal's office, do I?" His gaze slid past Patrick to the walkway beyond. "Hello, Mrs. Giardino. How are you doing?"

She nodded and stopped close, but not too close, to Patrick. "Have you found out anything about my son?"

"Maybe we should go inside to discuss this. Where it's warmer."

They trooped silently back to the room. In the men's absence, Stacy had made the bed and picked up the scattered clothes. Patrick relaxed a little. Not having the evidence of their indiscretion staring them all in the face helped a little. Stacy sat on the side of the bed and the two men took the chairs at the table. "Have you found my son?" she asked. "Have you found Carlo?"

Sullivan shook his head. "Marshal Thompson asked us to locate a ranch that belongs to Abel Giardino. We've found a place we think might be his and we've put it under surveillance."

"What have you seen? Have you seen a child?"

"We've only been watching the place a few hours at this point, and so far there's been nothing to see."

"Where is this place?" Stacy asked. "Can we go there?"

"That wouldn't be a good idea," Patrick said. "If they are holding Carlo and we go busting in, they might harm him—or carry him away to an even more remote location."

"As long as there aren't any signs that the boy is in danger, it's best to watch and figure out when to make our move," Sullivan said. "The first step is to verify that Carlo is even there."

"That's all you can tell me?" she asked. "We have to wait?"

"Maybe we'll know more later this morning, when people on the ranch wake up and start moving about. One of our spotters might see something then."

"You'll let me know right away?"

"We'll let you know as soon as it's safe to do so."

Patrick wanted to reach out, to squeeze her hand and offer her some sort of comfort. But with Sullivan looking on, he didn't dare. "Is there anything else you can tell us?" he asked.

"We did learn more about the wills," Sullivan said. "Both Sam's and Sam Junior's." He pulled a small notebook from his pocket and flipped through it. "We were able to get a judge to unseal the documents and they proved very interesting."

"How interesting?" Patrick asked. The hair on the back of his neck rose, a sure sign that the information was going to be good.

"Both Sammy and his father left everything to Carlo.

But it's tied up in a complicated trust. The manager of the trust directs the distribution of the money until Carlo is twenty-one."

"Who's the manager of the trust?" Stacy asked.

"You are." Sullivan closed the notebook and replaced it in his pocket. "You didn't know?"

She shook her head. "Why would Sam—or Sammy, for that matter—give me control over any of his money?"

"You're the boy's mother," Sullivan said. "Aren't you the most logical choice?"

"In the Giardino family, women never control the money," Stacy said.

"Was this one more way Sam was getting a dig in at Sammy?" Patrick asked. "It made sense that he'd die before his son, and then Sammy would have to watch while his son inherited everything—and you had control."

"Sammy would have hated that," Stacy said. "But Sammy had a will, too. Why didn't his will name someone else as administrator for the trust?"

"Maybe Sam forced him to agree to the same terms," Patrick said. "It seems to me that Sammy did what Sam told him to, at least some of the time." He'd married Stacy because his father had arranged it, hadn't he?

She nodded. "But this…"

"He may have had something else in mind," Sullivan said.

They both looked to him. He waited, clearly enjoying the suspense. "The terms of the trust make clear the custodian can do anything with the trust—including signing over control to a third party. Maybe Sammy figured he'd persuade you—or force you—to sign control over to him after his father died. And if he died first, his father could do the same."

"What happens to the trust if I die?" she asked.

"Control goes to Carlo's legal guardian."

"Do you have a will?" Patrick asked. "Have you named a guardian in the case of your death?"

She shook her head. "I'm only twenty-four. I never thought…"

Patrick did touch her hand then, moved by her distress. "It's all right," he said. "Of course you didn't."

"In lieu of a named guardian, it would be up to the court to decide," Sullivan said.

"Wouldn't the court give the boy to his next of kin?" Patrick asked.

"Maybe," Sullivan said. "Who would that be?"

"Not Uncle Abel," Stacy said. "I'd think it would be Elizabeth. She's his aunt."

"That could explain why the kidnappers decided they needed you alive," Patrick said. "Abel might have known enough about the will to know Carlo would receive everything. Later, he found out he'd need you to sign over control to him, so he sent his men back to get you."

"Why go to so much trouble?" she asked. "Abel has money of his own. And the government is liable to seize all of Sam's assets, aren't they?"

"The government can only seize assets they can link to crimes," Sullivan said. "And money we can get to and know about. Though we are still conducting our investigations, we suspect Sam had considerable amounts stashed in foreign accounts, in Switzerland and the Caymans, for example."

"So by gaining control of Carlo's trust, Abel Giardino could gain control of that money," Patrick said.

"Or someone else who is controlling Abel could gain control of the money," Sullivan said.

"But they need me alive, and they need Carlo alive, to do it," Stacy said. She didn't quite smile, but her eyes held a new light, and Patrick felt an easing of the tension within himself, also.

"So we can be reasonably sure the boy is safe for now," Sullivan said. "Which gives us more time to connect the dots between Giardino and our chief suspect."

"Senator Nordley," Patrick said.

Sullivan frowned and cut his eyes to Stacy. Clearly, he didn't approve of Stacy knowing of the government's interest in Nordley. "Yes, we would like to know more about the senator's involvement in this."

"Wait a minute." Stacy leaned toward him, her eyes blazing. "What exactly are you saying?"

Sullivan faced her, hands on his knees, his voice just this side of patronizing. "I'm saying we believe your son is safe with his uncle for the time being. The best thing for you to do is to go home and wait and we'll let you know when he can return to you."

Chapter Twelve

Stacy had heard of people seeing red, but she'd never experienced this red haze of anger clouding her vision. "My son is not *safe* with anyone but me. And you are insane if you think I'm going to go anywhere and wait until the government decides they can get around to returning him to me."

"He's in no danger," Sullivan said. "As long as he's safe…"

"How do you know that? You told me earlier you hadn't even seen him. Or was that a lie to try to shut me up?" She stood, and Patrick rose also, prepared to prevent her from launching herself at Sullivan. "He is away from his mother, with people he doesn't know. He's alone and afraid and you will not leave him there one *second* more than necessary."

"Mrs. Giardino, we are talking about a major investigation that has ramifications with the security of the United States," Sullivan said.

"What does Nordley have to do with national security?" Patrick asked.

"He's head of the Senate's committee on homeland security."

"I don't care if he's best friends with the head of the

Taliban," Stacy said. "You can investigate him *after* you rescue my son."

"We really can't do that." Sullivan looked to Patrick. "Explain to her how important this is."

"I can't." Patrick folded his arms over his chest. "You can't justify leaving a three-year-old in a dangerous situation for the convenience of an investigation."

"He's not in any danger."

"I don't agree. And I won't go along with any plan to delay his rescue."

"Then it's just as well the decision isn't up to you." Sullivan stood also and started for the door.

"Where are you going?" Stacy asked.

"Back to do my job. I'll be in touch."

"That's all you have to say?" Patrick asked.

"All that you need to know."

"Have you seen Carlo?" Stacy asked. "Is he really all right?"

Sullivan looked from one to the other. "I'm not going to discuss this investigation with you any further. Now, if you'll excuse me, I have a job to do."

"I have a job with this investigation, too," Patrick said. "The Bureau isn't running this show."

"It is now. But don't worry—you still have a role. Your job is to protect Mrs. Giardino." He smirked. "Obviously, you're taking that assignment very seriously." He opened the door. "I'll be in touch."

Sullivan left. Patrick moved to the window and watched the agent get into a black SUV and drive away.

Stacy watched over Patrick's shoulder. "Aren't you going to stop him?" she asked.

"I can't." He turned away from the window. "That

last dig about you was his way of letting me know he won't say anything to my supervisors about our relationship as long as I stay out of his way. If I make trouble, he'll have me reassigned. You'll get a new handler who'll have orders not to let you get near the investigation."

"I can't believe this is happening. What are we going to do?"

"At least if I stay with you we can work together." He put his arm around her and pulled her close. "We'll find Carlo."

"But he ordered you to stay away."

"It wouldn't be the first time I've bent the rules to help someone I was sworn to protect." He'd sent Elizabeth Giardino a gun, though doing so had been out of line. Directly disobeying orders to look for Carlo was a much more serious transgression; it could cost him his career.

"You'd risk your job for me?" she asked.

"Finding Carlo is the right thing to do," he said.

"How will we find him? We don't know where the ranch is."

"The same way Sullivan probably found him—we'll talk to people and listen to what they have to say. We will find him, Stacy. I promise." He squeezed her shoulder. And when they did, he'd do what he had to do to reunite the child with his mother, even if it meant defying his bosses and the government.

Stacy dressed in the clothes she'd worn the day before, which were at least a little cleaner after their soak in the tub and a night spent drying over a chair. Patrick wore clothes that had belonged to the pale-eyed man, though the shirt was a little tight across his broader shoulders. They packed their few belongings into Pale Eyes's suitcase and prepared to leave. They were on their way out the door when Stacy remembered the other suitcase. She put her hand on Patrick's arm to stop him. "Wait. What about the money?"

He nodded and went to retrieve the second case from under the bed. He unzipped the top and surveyed the neat stacks of bills inside, as if to reassure himself they were still there.

"We didn't tell Sullivan about this," she said.

"I never told my office, either." The oversight wasn't deliberate; he'd simply forgotten with everything else that had happened. He zipped up the case. "I'll be sure to report it the next time Sullivan bothers to get in touch. In the meantime, we might be able to use it as a bargaining chip."

"With the feds or with Uncle Abel?" she asked.

"Maybe both." He carried the case out to the car and locked it in the trunk. He didn't know if fifty thousand dollars was enough to persuade anyone involved in this case to act differently, but the money might link up some of the players. Had the two thugs been delivering or receiving the cash? Who had put it into that suitcase? He added these to the growing list of unanswered questions in this case.

LIGHT SNOW FELL as they drove toward Crested Butte. Stacy didn't ask what they'd do when they got there. Stacy trusted Patrick had a plan. All she could focus on was Carlo and praying that he was indeed all right. Maybe Abel and Willa liked little children and they'd be kind to him and do what they could to calm his fears. It wasn't the same as having his mother with him, but she wanted him to feel safe. To know he was loved. Wasn't that the best security of all, to know that someone cared about you and wanted to protect you?

"Do you think Agent Sullivan is right about the reason Carlo was kidnapped?" she asked. "To gain control of the money?"

"Greed motivates a lot of crimes. But you said Abel has money of his own?"

"Sam always said he did. He referred to him as 'my brother, the rich rancher.'"

"What kind of ranch does he have? Cattle?"

"Horses, I think. Maybe some cattle, too. I'm not sure. Sam always talked about Abel 'playing cowboy' and said he was rolling in the big bucks."

"Maybe he was being sarcastic."

"Maybe. An honest rancher probably doesn't have as much money as a mobster."

"We don't know that he's honest," Patrick said.

"Kidnapping isn't honest," she agreed. "And if he was the one who sent those two thugs after us in the canyon, how did he know to hire people who had worked for Sam, unless he and Sam had been in contact—even working together—all along?"

"I wonder if the cash in that suitcase was payment to the thugs for going after you—or if they were supposed to deliver it to Abel from someone else."

"From Senator Nordley?" she asked. "Was he fronting cash to Abel until he had the money from the will?"

Patrick shook his head. "It's all speculation. And we

could be completely wrong. We're still not certain Abel even has Carlo."

She slid down lower in the seat. "I hope he does. At least then we know where he is. If he isn't with Abel and Willa, then he's vanished." The thought made it difficult to breathe.

Patrick squeezed her hand. "We'll find him. I promise."

She nodded, too moved to speak. She believed he meant his words, but she also knew he couldn't guarantee that Carlo was safe. She wouldn't rest easy again until her son was safe in her arms, and far away from the people who wanted to hurt him or use him.

After two hours of driving, a highway sign informed them they had reached the outskirts of Crested Butte. Patrick turned off the highway at a complex of warehouses and industrial-supply businesses. "I'm headed to the airport," he said, before Stacy could ask. "We need to get rid of this car."

"Because Abel's men might recognize it?"

He glanced at her. "That, and because the feds know it."

She sat back in her seat. Right. If Sullivan and his bunch recognized that Stacy and Patrick were getting too close to their precious investigation, they'd do everything they could to stop them.

Patrick parked the car at Crested Butte's tiny airport, which was housed in a single terminal with two gates. He carried their suitcases inside and led the way to the rental car counter, where he rented a yellow Jeep Cherokee with a ski rack. "The snow is great right now," the clerk said as she handed over the keys. "Have a great vacation."

"Thanks." His eyes met Stacy's and she looked away. She only wished they were a happy couple on a relaxing vacation, instead of two people thrown together in a desperate search for her missing son.

From the airport they drove into the heart of Crested Butte, which proved to be a picturesque hamlet of Victorian-era wood-front buildings painted bright colors, clustered along a few streets against a backdrop of snow-covered mountains. Patrick found the courthouse, parked in front of it and went inside to the clerk's office. "We're doing some research and would like to look through the tax records," he told the middle-aged redhead behind the counter.

"You can use this computer." The clerk led them to a small workstation and pulled up the county records program. "You can search by the name of the owner or by address," she said. She started to type in an example, but the phone rang. "I'd better get that," she said. "If you have any questions, just ask."

Stacy sat in the chair in front of the terminal while Patrick pulled a second chair alongside her. "I guess I'll start with the obvious," she said. She typed the word *Giardino* in the space for last name and hit Enter.

"No records returned," Patrick said.

In quick succession she tried Abel, Willa, Sam and even Carlo. But nothing came up that looked remotely like the ranch Abel supposedly owned. "Try Nordley," Patrick suggested.

She tried the name. "Nothing."

Patrick sat back. "This isn't getting us anywhere.

Even in a county this small, there must be thousands of properties. We can't research them all."

"You're right." She clicked back to the home page, then pushed out her chair. "I have an idea. Just give me a minute."

With her most friendly smile in place, she approached the clerk. "Maybe you can help me," she said. "I'm doing a college thesis on historic ranches of Gunnison County. Do you know who might have a listing of all the ranches in the area?"

The lines on the clerk's forehead deepened. "The historical society might be able to help you," she said.

"So you don't maintain any kind of listing of ranches or anything like that in this office?"

"We have a map the cattleman's society put together a couple years back, but it won't tell you if the places on it are historic or not."

"Could I see the map? It would be a great start."

"I think I have a copy around here somewhere." She retreated to a back room and returned a few minutes later with a yellowing scroll. "Here you go. Just return it to me when you're done."

Resisting the urge to unfurl the scroll and examine it right there at the counter, Stacy thanked the woman and carried her prize back to the workstation. "This map supposedly shows the ranches in the county," she said.

Patrick took hold of one end and helped her spread out the documents, which proved to be an artistic rendering of the county, complete with mountain ranges, miniature skiers and carefully sketched-in cattle and forests. Stacy scanned the names of the ranches: Red Hawk, Powderhorn Creek, Pogna Ranch. She stopped when she came to a name affixed to a parcel not far from town. "Willing and Able," she read. "That has to be it. It's a play on their names—Willa and Abel."

Patrick pulled out a notebook and wrote down the general location of the ranch. Stacy typed the road number into the computer and came up with a listing of properties in the vicinity. Third from the top was the name A.G. Holdings. "Abel Giardino," she said.

Patrick nodded and replaced the notebook in his coat. "Let's drive out there and take a look."

Stacy returned the map to the clerk. "Did you find what you were looking for?" the woman asked.

"I think so. Thank you very much." She couldn't hold back her smile. Maybe in just a little while she'd be able to see her son.

"Hurry," she said to Patrick, and rushed past him toward the Jeep.

He followed at a slower pace. Once they were buckled in, he turned to her before he started the car. "Right now we're just going to drive by to make sure we have the right location—and to see if we spot any of the federal surveillance. I doubt we will—these guys are very good. But we won't be stopping and lingering. And we won't be driving up to the front door and demanding to see Carlo."

"Of course not." Though part of her had envisioned just such a scenario.

"I know it's hard for you, being this close and having to wait," he said. "But if we're going to retrieve Carlo safely, we have to have a plan. I'm hoping this drive will suggest a way to approach the ranch house without being seen by either the feds or Abel's guards. This is just a reconnaissance mission."

She nodded. "All right." She reached out and pressed down the door lock. She could do this—but if she actually saw Carlo, all bets were off.

Patrick consulted the map of the area the rental car company had given him, then drove out of town and turned onto a plowed gravel road that cut between expanses of snow-covered fields crisscrossed with sagging barbed-wire fencing. They passed herds of cattle eating hay that ranchers had spread for them that morning, the feed a dark green line against the pristine whiteness of the snow that rose above the animals' hocks.

Other pastures were vacant, the snow as smooth as buttercream frosting on a wedding cake, unmarred by even the tracks of deer. Stacy thought again of the remoteness and loneliness of this country. "I could never live here," she said. "So far from everything."

"Some people like it, I guess," he said. "No neighbors to see what you're up to."

No neighbors to notice a little boy who didn't belong there. "Our neighbors in New York probably saw plenty," she said. "But they knew to keep their mouths shut."

"Good point." Patrick shifted into a lower gear to climb a steep hill. "The Willing and Able should be up ahead, just around this curve."

Stacy looked, but saw nothing but the same empty fields and barbed wire. They drove for another five minutes before a driveway appeared, a simple W&A on the black iron gate, which was closed, though the packed snow showed signs of recent travel up the drive. Stacy craned her neck, but could see nothing past the line of trees that marked a bend in the driveway. She tried to suppress her disappointment. "I thought we'd at least see a house or something." A house with a little boy's face pressed to the window, watching for his mother.

"These ranch houses are set way off the road," Patrick said. "I figured the best we could do would be to get a sense of the layout and determine the most likely locations for federal agents."

"And what did you decide?" she asked.

"I think the feds probably have someone watching the gate," he said. "There's another drive across the road. My guess someone is set up in the trees."

"Do you think they recognized us?" Her stomach lurched.

"I ducked my head and yours was turned away. They might run a check on the Jeep's plate and they'll find out it's a rental, but I used a fake ID."

A surprised laugh escaped her lips. "You have a fake ID?"

The tips of his ears flushed red. "It comes in handy sometimes."

"And here I thought you were a strictly-by-the-book guy."

"I do what I have to to protect my charges."

She reached out and squeezed his hand. "Thank you for protecting me. And thank you for staying with me after Sullivan found out about us. I know you didn't have to do that."

"I won't leave you until I know you're safe."

But he would leave her then. The knowledge started an ache deep in her chest. When had this man, whom she had hated, even feared when they first met, become such an important part of her life? The shift in her attitude had happened long before they'd slept together; something in her had recognized Marshal Patrick Thompson as someone she could depend on. Someone she could trust with her deepest secrets.

With her heart.

She pushed the idea away. She had to think about Carlo now, to focus on him. Everything else, including worries about the future, was secondary to freeing Carlo and keeping him safe. "How are we going to get to the ranch house and find Carlo?" she asked.

"We'll have to find a back way in."

"How are we going to do that?"

"I have some ideas. But first, let's get out of here."

He turned onto another gravel road marked with a green Forest Service sign. After crawling along for what seemed to Stacy like an hour, they emerged onto the highway south of town. "We need to rent a hotel room," Patrick said. "We can talk there without being overheard and make plans."

"All right." Renting a room meant more delays, but so would arguing with him. And when they did find Carlo, it would be good to have a safe, warm room to bring him back to.

They found a vacancy at a small motel in town but didn't bother to bring their luggage inside. They did bring the map, which Patrick spread out on the table by the window. "This is the road we came in on," he showed her, tracing the route with his finger.

"There's the ranch." She pointed to the curve near the ranch gate.

"Right. Now, let's see...." He punched some buttons on his phone, then turned the screen so she could see.

She studied the photo of one large roof and several smaller ones grouped among some trees. "What am I looking at?" she asked.

"That's the Google Earth shot of the Willing and Able ranch house."

"You're kidding."

He shook his head. "Forget government satellites. Anyone can look at this stuff online."

"I wonder if Abel knows that."

"Even if he does, there's nothing he can do to prevent it." He laid the phone alongside the map and zoomed out. "This picture was taken in the summer. You can see this back drive that snakes behind the house and out this other direction." He pointed to a faint, broken line on the map. "That's this road here."

"It's not really a road," she said. "More of a trail."

"But it's a way in."

"Except it's probably not plowed in the winter."

"If it is, the feds will have it staked out. But if it isn't, they probably won't bother watching it too closely."

"But that doesn't help us. Even with four-wheel drive we won't get down a road that hasn't been plowed. You saw how deep the snow was."

"We can't drive down it. But we can walk. Or rather, snowshoe."

"Uncle Abel's men will spot us a mile off. It's not as if we can run in snowshoes."

"We'll wait until after dark. They won't see us. And we won't have to run."

"Carlo could never walk far through snow, and he's almost too big for me to carry."

"I could carry him."

She studied the image of the ranch house roof. Was Carlo really there? "I don't know. Can we really do this?"

"We can. I think it's the best way to get close and remain undetected. Once we determine where he is in the house, we'll sneak in and out with as little fuss as possible."

She regarded him more closely. "You talk as if you've done this kind of thing before."

"I was with Special Forces in the service."

"You're just full of surprises, aren't you?"

"Before long you're going to know all my secrets," he said. He didn't exactly smile, but the look he gave her sent a jolt of heat straight to her belly.

"How can I say no when you put it like that?" She took a deep breath. "What next?"

"We need better winter clothing, snowshoes and a few other supplies. Time to go shopping."

Good idea. Shopping was one thing she was good at, and searching through stores for the supplies they needed would eat up time and provide a welcome distraction from her worries about Carlo and the chances of this crazy plan succeeding.

At a backcountry outfitter around the corner from their hotel they purchased long underwear, snow pants and jackets, hats, mittens and snowshoes. "These have a narrower profile that make walking and even running easier than ever," the clerk, a young man with a goatee and two earrings, pointed out as he helped Stacy strap on the lightweight aluminum shoes. "And you'll want poles to help with your balance." He shortened a pair of aluminum poles and handed them to her.

She stood in the middle of the store, poles planted on either side of her, and looked over at Patrick. He was busy stuffing their purchases into a large backpack. "I think I can get the hang of this," she said.

"Trust me," the clerk said. "If you can walk, you can snowshoe."

From the outfitters, they walked down the sidewalk between walls of snow, past shops that sold everything from T-shirts to gourmet cookware. "Are we looking for anything in particular?" she asked.

"Right now we're just killing time," he said. "If you see anyplace you want to go into, say the word."

She stopped in front of a window that displayed a variety of toys from an old-fashioned sled to video games. "Let's go in here," she said.

The store was filled with items that would have delighted Carlo, but she settled on a ten-inch-high bear with thick brown fur and a blue bow around its neck. "I think he would like this," she said. When they took him back to the hotel later tonight—as she prayed they would—it would be good to give him this bear to comfort and distract him.

"I'm sure he would," Patrick said, and took out his wallet to pay for the purchase.

They ate pizza at a restaurant at one end of the street. "Do you think Sullivan was right, that Carlo is safe?" she asked as she nibbled a slice of pepperoni.

"I think he didn't want you to know at first that

they'd found the boy, but I think he is safe. Abel needs Carlo to have access to the money."

"How does Senator Nordley play into this?"

"Rumor has it he wants to run for president. That takes a lot of money. Maybe Abel promised Nordley a share of the cash if he'd help Abel get his hands on it."

"He can have every bit of it, for all I care. I just want my son safely back with me. I don't even want the Giardinos' ill-gotten gains."

"Seems to me you've earned your share of their wealth," he said. "It could make you and Carlo a lot more comfortable."

"I can look after Carlo myself," she said. "I'd rather be poor and free of the taint of that family. I'm even thinking of changing my name when this is all over."

"Back to your maiden name?" he asked.

She made a face. "It's my father's name, and he never did me any favors. I think I'll have to come up with something new. A fresh start."

"If you go into WITSEC, you can choose whatever name you like." At her frown, he held up his hand. "I know you don't want to go into the program, but I just thought I'd point out that it automatically comes with a name change, and a fresh start."

"I'll think about it." Maybe it wouldn't be so bad, letting the government help hcr out. And it might mean she'd get to continue to see Patrick, at least some of the time.

After lunch they slowly made their way up the other side of the street to the hotel. Back in their room, she flopped down on the bed. "This waiting is killing me. When can we leave?"

"It gets dark pretty early. We can start that way about four-thirty."

She checked the bedside clock. "Three hours."

"Try to get some sleep. It could be a long night."

"What are you going to do?"

"I'm going to organize our gear." Already he'd spread half their purchases on the table and was unwrapping items—a flashlight, energy bars, water bottles, first aid kit, emergency blanket and more things she couldn't remember.

"You can lie down on the bed and I promise I won't attack you," she said.

He looked startled. "What?"

"I know you feel bad about us sleeping together," she said. "Like you shirked your duty or betrayed an oath or something."

"You're wrong." He went back to wrestling with the wrapping on a small pair of binoculars. "I ought to feel bad about my unprofessional behavior, but I can't regret making love to you."

"Then why are you avoiding even touching me?"

He set aside the binoculars and looked at her. "Because if I touch you—if I come over there and lie down beside you—I won't be content with just a nap."

"Oh." His words—and the heated look in his eyes when he said them—sent a hot shiver down to her toes.

"You must be exhausted," he said. "You're worried about your son and nervous about tonight. Sex is probably the last thing on your mind. I'm trying to be a gentleman."

She was all those things he'd said, but none of that

mattered now. "I don't need a gentleman right now," she said. "I just need you."

His silence was like a vise around her chest, preventing her from breathing. Maybe she'd been wrong to be so frank, so open with him. Maybe he didn't really want her that way. He was trying to find a kind way to reject her.

He stood, his gaze still locked to hers, and unbuttoned the top button of his shirt. "I never was good at being a gentleman," he said.

Chapter Thirteen

Whereas their lovemaking before had been full of the uncertainties and hesitations of any new partners, Stacy felt more sure of herself with Patrick now—and more sure of him as a man who would welcome whatever she had to offer. When they lay together, naked under the covers, she allowed herself the luxury of exploring his body—of discovering the play of muscle beneath the smooth flesh of his back and shoulders, delighting in the ticklish spot just at his waist, thrilling to the feel of the shadow of beard along his jaw.

"What is this?" she asked, running her finger along a puckered scar across the top of one hip.

"Sniper round."

"And this?" She moved to a purple slash across his biceps.

"Bullet wound." He covered her hand with his. "If you start inventorying my scars, we'll be here all night."

His kiss cut off her response, but the kiss was response enough. She'd never known such kisses, deep and sweet, both insistent and tender, leaving her dizzy and breathless and feeling so…cherished. She opened her eyes and met his gaze.

"I like that you watch me when we make love," he said.

"I don't want to miss anything," he said. With Sammy—before he'd turned his back on her altogether—she'd kept her eyes closed to avoid seeing the disdain with which he so often regarded her. Patrick's eyes held none of that scorn—only lust and longing and something that felt, to her at least, like appreciation.

They made love languidly that afternoon, each giving and receiving pleasure, teasing out the moments until they could wait no longer. After he entered her, she urged him onto his back so that she rode atop him, directing the tempo and depth of his strokes, his hands guiding her hips, the increasing pace of his breathing and the glazed look in his eyes letting her know when he was near to losing control. But he turned the tables when he reached down to touch her, sending her over the edge with a cry of delight.

Afterward, they lay together, cocooned in warmth and satisfaction, the light showing through the crack between the curtains fading from gold to muddy gray. "No tears this time," he said.

"No tears." She had plenty to cry about in her life right now, but Patrick was not one of those things. She might weep later, when he left her. But not now. She wouldn't spoil the time they had together with sorrow.

PATRICK HADN'T INTENDED to fall asleep, but he must have. When he woke it was full dark, the only light the faint glow from the parking lot security lights. Stacy lay curled against him. He shook her gently. "Stacy. It's time to go."

She stirred and buried her head deeper under the covers. "Stacy!" He shook her harder. "It's time to get up and go find Carlo."

"Carlo." She looked up at him, then sat up, pushing off the covers. "What time is it?"

He checked the clock. "It's after six."

"Oh, no! We're late!" She scrambled out of bed and grabbed for her clothes.

"It's okay." He moved to the table and began searching through their purchases. "We have plenty of time. Waiting until later is probably better. Don't forget to dress warm."

"All of a sudden I'm so nervous," she said. "What if we can't find him? What if the feds stop us? Or Abel and his men?"

"Stacy, it's okay." He put his hand on her shoulder. "It will be all right. You can do this."

Her eyes met his and some of the panic faded. She nodded. "You're right. Together, we can do this."

Half an hour later, they were headed out of town in the Jeep, the headlights cutting through the darkness. He took a different route this time, one he'd plotted on the map to avoid the locations where federal agents were most likely to be posted. This meant traveling at slow speeds down narrow, winding back roads. Stacy didn't say a word, but she gripped the dashboard as they bumped over ruts, tension radiating from her.

After more than an hour, they passed a break in the fence. Patrick stopped, then backed up the Jeep and angled it until the headlights shone through the gap, illuminating the faint indentations of a snow-clogged track. He checked the GPS coordinates on his phone. "This is where we get out," he said.

"Are we just going to leave the Jeep here?" she asked.

"I think I can nose it under those trees ahead. I doubt anyone is going to come along at this time of night. There aren't any fresh tracks since the snow this morning."

He parked the car under the trees and they piled out and strapped on snowshoes. Stacy took a few experimental steps forward. "What do you think?" Patrick asked.

"Not bad," she said. "Hopefully I'll do as well in deep snow." She tilted her head to look up at the sky. The morning's clouds had vanished, leaving inky black sky dotted with a million stars and a thin sliver of moon. "It's beautiful," she said, her breath forming a cloud.

"Beautiful, but cold." He moved alongside her and handed her a pair of chemical heat packs. "Slip these into your mittens."

"Thanks." She added the hot packs to her mittens, then switched on the headlamp he'd also handed her. "We've got about a mile trek to the ranch house," he said. "We'll take it slow, and no talking. I don't think anyone's listening, but might as well be safe."

"What if they have dogs?"

"They aren't likely to be roaming around away from the house in this cold. We'll be on the lookout when we get closer. Are you ready?"

"Yes. Let's go."

He led the way down the snow-packed trail. Their tracks would have been clearly visible to anyone who passed by, but there was no way he could think of to hide their passage in the fresh snow. He set a brisk pace, but soon slowed as Stacy fell farther and farther behind. He stopped and waited for her to catch up. "I'm sorry," she whispered. "I—"

He put a finger to his lips and shook his head, then handed her a bottle of water. She drank, then he drank and replaced the bottle in the pack and patted her shoulder. *You're doing great,* he wanted to tell her. Instead, he gave her a thumbs-up and indicated they should move on.

He shortened his steps and she was better able to match his pace. The track emerged from the woods into open pasture and the drifts grew deeper, their shoes sinking into the soft, untrodden snow. Clearly, no one had passed this way in some time—a good indication that the feds had overlooked this route, too.

After about half an hour they saw the glow from the lights of the house, then they rounded a curve in the trail and spotted the house itself, surrounded by half a dozen outbuildings—horse stalls, a garage and storage sheds. Patrick stopped and she halted behind him, close enough he could hear her labored breathing.

He waited, listening for the barks of dogs or the rev of an engine, for shouts or voices or any indication that they'd been spotted. He pulled the binoculars from the inside of his jacket and scanned the area, wishing for the night-vision goggles he'd used in the military. Still, the outside security lights provided enough illumination for him to determine that the area was deserted.

They were going to have to get a lot closer to the

house to find the boy. He touched Stacy's shoulder and indicated they should remove their snowshoes.

Snowshoes discarded and poles laid aside, he started toward the house, keeping to the shadows, stepping in snow to his knees. Stacy literally followed in his footsteps. Though the snow made for slow going, it also muffled the sound of their approach. The house remained silent, undisturbed by their presence.

He stopped at the edge of the clearing, about a hundred yards from the side of the house, giving them a view of both the front and back yards. Nothing moved, and the only sounds were the hum of what must be a furnace and the rough inhalation and exhalation of their own breath.

Stacy tugged on his arm and he bent to her. She put her mouth against his ear. "The curtains are all closed," she said. "How are we going to know which room Carlo is in? And how are we going to get to him?"

His original plan had been to hunker down and watch the house until he had a feel for the layout, but arriving so late, they could sit here all night and be no better informed in the morning than they were now. And the longer they stayed, the greater the risk of someone spotting the Jeep or seeing their tracks heading toward the house.

He turned and led her back down the trail until they were far enough away from the house he was sure they wouldn't be heard. "We'll have to get inside," he said.

"How? The doors will be locked, and there will be guards."

"I can pick a lock. But I don't think there will be guards."

"Sam always had bodyguards," she said.

"But Abel isn't Sam. He's a rancher, not a mobster. And there aren't enough vehicles for very many people to be here. That garage holds two cars, at most, and the only other car is that old truck by the shed—and it's covered in snow, as if it hasn't been driven in weeks."

"Maybe they're parked somewhere else."

"Maybe so, but why go to all that trouble? This is Abel's home. He feels safe here. If he does have guards, they're probably up by the main gate—the only way in this time of year."

"It's still taking a huge risk."

"Would you rather we went away and left Carlo in there?"

"No. Of course not."

"Good. Then follow me inside. Stick close and don't make a sound. From what I could see, there's a front door, a side door opening to the walkway to the garage and a back door that probably opens into a kitchen or a mudroom."

"That's all I saw, too."

"We'll try the back door first. If we hear anything, we'll move to another door, or a window."

"What do we do when we find Carlo?"

"If he's alone, we'll sneak him out the same way we came in. If he isn't alone, I'll take care of the guard and you look after Carlo. If we're separated, meet up back at the Jeep."

"All right." She hesitated, then stood on tiptoe and kissed his cheek. "Thank you," she whispered. "For everything."

She should wait and thank him when her boy was

safe, but he didn't tell her that, merely patted her shoulder then turned to lead the way up to the house. He'd deliberately downplayed the risk of what they were about to do, in order not to frighten her, but he had no such delusions. It would take all his skills—and a great deal of luck—to come out of this unscathed.

STACY FOLLOWED PATRICK out of the shadows onto the pristine expanse of snow behind the ranch house. Their footsteps made dark holes in the snow, like a row of ellipses leading across the yard. At the bottom of the steps they halted and listened. The furnace shut off abruptly and she strained her ears, listening. From somewhere deep inside the house came the sound of voices, followed by the buzz of canned laughter—the television.

Patrick wiped his feet on the bottom steps and brushed the bottoms of his trousers, trying to remove as much snow as possible. She did the same. His eyes met hers and he nodded, then started up the steps.

The knob turned easily in his hand. Maybe he'd been right about Abel not thinking like a criminal; Sam would never have left a door unlocked, especially not at night.

Her heart hammered painfully as he eased open the door, then slipped inside, moving gracefully despite the bulky pack on his back. A few seconds later, he beckoned for her to follow.

A light over the stove cast a dim glow over scuffed red linoleum floors and white Formica countertops. A dish drainer with four plates, four forks, three glasses and a coffee cup sat beside the sink. She felt a jolt of elation as she counted the dishes. If one of the sets belonged to Carlo, that meant they had only three adults to deal with.

A door from the kitchen led into a darkened dining room. Patrick stopped to one side of the doorway and pulled her alongside him. From here they could look into the living room, where a man and an older woman sat in two armchairs in front of a large flat-screen television. She scanned the room for some sign of Carlo but found none.

They retreated to the kitchen and moved to a second door, which opened into a cramped hallway and a flight of stairs leading straight up. Patrick started up them, keeping close to the railing. She did the same, trying to make each step as light and soundless as possible.

At the top of the stairs they stopped again to listen. A commercial came on the television advertising a fast-food chain. "Is there any more of that ice cream?" a man's voice asked.

"In the freezer," a woman answered. "Get me a bowl, too."

Stacy clung to the stair railing, feeling dizzy. Floor-boards creaked below them as the man moved from the living room into the kitchen, where only seconds before, he would have found them. Light poured out from the room as he flicked the switch and she couldn't breathe. Would he notice anything out of place in the room? Despite their best efforts, had they tracked snow inside?

Patrick's hand on her arm forced her attention back to him. He indicated they should continue down the hallway to the left of the stairs. On tiptoe, she followed, toward a door beneath which a light glowed.

The light in the kitchen went out as they reached the

doorway that must lead to a bedroom. Patrick put his ear to the door, and she moved past him to do the same.

A woman was speaking. Stacy gasped as she recognized *Where the Wild Things Are,* one of Carlo's favorite books. "'Oh, please don't go—we'll eat you up—we love you so!'"

"That's my favorite part," a little boy answered.

Stacy bit her thumb to keep from crying out. Patrick put a steadying hand on her shoulder. She nodded, though it took everything in her not to burst in and grab her child to her. She looked to Patrick, her eyes pleading. *What do we do?* she mouthed.

He gestured they should wait.

The minutes dragged as she listened to the woman finish reading the story. Had the book really been so long when she'd read it? When Max was finally safely home the woman pronounced, "The end."

"Read it again," Carlo said when she was done. The way he always did when Stacy read that story to him.

"It's time for you to go to sleep now," the woman said.

"Will I see Mommy tomorrow?" Carlo asked.

Stacy let out a moan—she couldn't help it. Patrick gripped her shoulder more tightly and she nodded.

"Maybe your mommy will come tomorrow," the woman said. "Now close your eyes and go to sleep."

"I want a drink of water first."

Patrick stiffened and moved to the other side of the door. Stacy stepped farther into the shadows on her side.

Steps crossed the room, then the doorknob turned and a shaft of light fell on the hallway floor. A short, middle-aged woman with long gray hair stepped out into the hallway. Before Stacy could even blink, Patrick clamped his hand over the woman's mouth and carried her into the bathroom across the hall. Stacy slipped into the bedroom.

"Mama!" Carlo shouted.

"Shh! Shh!" She put her fingers to her lips and rushed to him. "You have to be very quiet," she said. "I don't want Uncle Abel to know I'm here."

The boy frowned. "Why not?"

"It's a surprise." She tucked the blanket from his bed around him and gathered him into her arms. He wore blue flannel pajamas with little fire trucks on them and she could smell toothpaste on his breath. "I've missed you so much," she whispered, hugging him tightly.

"I've missed you, too. Where have you been?"

"Shh. We can't talk now. Now, promise me you'll be very, very quiet. A friend and I are going to take you snowshoeing in the woods. Won't that be fun?"

"But it's dark." He looked toward the window. "And it's cold."

"Please, baby, it will be all right, I promise. Just be quiet and do what Mommy tells you."

"Uncle Abel and Grandma Willa won't like it," he said.

She hesitated. How could she explain the danger to a three-year-old? "No, they won't like it," she said. "And if they catch Mommy here with you, they might hurt us both. So it's very important that we sneak away without them knowing."

Unfortunately, this information only confused the boy more. "But Uncle Abel told me you were coming to see me soon. And he promised to take me for a ride on one of his horses."

"Maybe you can do that soon." She tucked the blanket more firmly around him. "Do you have snow boots?"

"Downstairs."

They didn't have time to search downstairs for boots. She settled for pulling a pair of socks over his bare feet.

The bedroom door opened and Patrick stuck his head in. "We need to go," he whispered.

"Carlo, this is my friend, Patrick," Stacy said. "He's going snowshoeing with us."

Carlo's eyes widened. "He's big."

"Hello, Carlo," Patrick said. "Will you let me carry you?"

Carlo shook his head and clung to his mother.

"I'd better take him for now," she said.

He held the door open wider and motioned for her to go ahead of him.

The kitchen was still dark and the television still blared as they made their way down the stairs. Carlo squirmed and buried his head against Stacy's shoulder, but didn't say a word. She pulled the blanket up over his head and stepped carefully down the stairs. Only a few more steps and they'd be out of the house, halfway to safety.

At the bottom of the stairs, Patrick moved ahead of her. He kept one hand in his pocket and she was sure he was holding his gun. She wondered what he'd done with the babysitter but would have to wait to ask him.

They crossed the kitchen, but when he pulled on the

door, it refused to yield. He turned the knob back and forth, but the door wouldn't budge.

"I remembered to lock it this time," said a voice behind him. "Now turn around, slowly. And keep your hands where I can see them."

Chapter Fourteen

"Uncle Abel, you weren't supposed to see us." Carlo's childish voice broke the silence of the adults, reminding Patrick of all that was at stake here, far beyond his own safety.

"Your uncle Abel is smarter than some people think," the older man said. He was clearly cut from the same mold as Sam Giardino, with the same putty nose and jowly chin, more fleshy and older looking than his brother, who had relied on plastic surgery and expensive spa treatments to maintain his youthful looks.

Abel gestured with his pistol. "Young man, take that gun out of your pocket and lay it on the counter there."

Patrick did as he asked.

"I won't let you take my son." Stacy shifted Carlo to one hip and glared at the old man.

"Your son is a Giardino. He belongs with family." The old woman moved slowly into the kitchen, pushing a walker in front of her. Her sparse gray hair was cut short like a man's and her spine was bent thirty degrees, but her voice was strong and her eyes blazed with determination.

"He belongs with his mother," Stacy declared.

The old woman's mouth twisted into an expression

of disgust. "Sam never should have let his son marry you. I knew as soon as I saw you at the wedding that you had no respect for the family. You were trash he never should have bothered picking up."

Stacy drew herself up taller, eyes sparking. If not for the boy in her arms, Patrick thought she might have flown at the woman. "Your family doesn't deserve my respect," she said.

The old woman dismissed her with a wave and turned to her son. "Get rid of the man and we'll deal with her later."

"I want to know who he is first." Abel jabbed the gun at Patrick. "Who sent you?"

"Nobody sent me," Patrick said. "I agreed to help Stacy retrieve her son."

"I told you, I'm not stupid." He waved the gun threateningly. "You're that marshal assigned to protect her. Thompson."

Patrick didn't allow his expression to betray his surprise. No one was supposed to know where Stacy had been since Sammy's death—or who she was with. Though maybe he had heard the speculation in the news. "My job is to keep her and the boy safe," he said. "I don't care about anything else."

"As if I'd believe that. You work for the feds. Though you've got more nerve than most of them, coming right into my house."

"He's telling the truth," Stacy said. "He's only here to help me. Let us go and we'll leave you alone."

"Shut up," the old woman snapped. "I told you, we'll deal with you later."

"I have something that belongs to you," Patrick said.

"Maybe we can agree to an exchange—the boy and Stacy for what I have."

"What do you have that belongs to me?"

"I have the fifty thousand dollars."

The old man arched one eyebrow. "Fifty thousand dollars that belongs to me? And where did you get that?"

"The two men you sent after us in the canyon had it."

"Those two idiots," Willa said. "I told Abel that was a bad idea. He thought we should get you out of the way and bring Stacy here by herself. You were doing fine getting here on your own without those two interfering, and we could have dealt with you when you arrived. But he doesn't listen to his mother."

Stacy stared at the old woman. Patrick could read her thoughts from the expression on her face—was the old lady for real?

"You probably think fifty thousand dollars is a lot of money to a man like me," Abel said.

"Fifty thousand dollars is a lot of money to most people," Patrick said.

"Not to my brother. If you offered fifty thousand dollars to Sam, he'd take it as an insult."

"I'm not offering the money to your brother," Patrick said. "I'm offering it to you."

"What do you think, Mother? Are those two worth fifty thousand dollars?"

"She isn't worth fifty cents to me, but she's not getting the boy for any price."

"Carlo is my son," Stacy said. "You have no claim on him."

"Stacy," Patrick said. He gave her a warning look. They had nothing to gain by antagonizing these people.

She bit her lip and gave a single nod to show she understood, then rested her head against Carlo's. He whispered something to her and she replied, then smoothed her hand down his back.

"Give me the money," Abel demanded, a new, harder edge to his voice.

"It isn't here," Patrick said. "You let Stacy and Carlo go and once they're safely away, I'll take you to the money."

"And then what am I supposed to do with you?" Abel grinned, showing a missing incisor. "I could kill you, but then I could do that anyway."

"Patrick, no!" Stacy said. "I won't leave without you."

"So that's how it goes, is it?" Abel's expression darkened. "My nephew not cold in his grave and you've taken up with a fed."

Willa called Stacy an obscene name. Stacy cradled Carlo's head to her breast, covering his ears.

"I think I will kill you," Abel said.

"Not in front of the boy," Willa admonished, as if she was warning him against drinking or swearing or some other petty sin.

"No, not in front of the boy," Abel agreed. He motioned to Patrick again. "Take off that pack and turn and face the door, hands behind your back."

Patrick did as the old man asked, moving as slowly as possible, but quickly enough not to provoke his captor. Stacy kept her eyes on him, anger and fear doing battle in her expression. "So you don't care about the money?" Patrick said, when he was facing the door.

"I wondered what happened to it, but there's plenty

more where that came from. Fifty thousand is nothing compared to what I'm going to have as soon as Stacy here signs a few papers for me."

"I won't sign anything unless you let Carlo go," she said.

"Carlo will be fine here with Mother and me. We'll love him like the son and grandson we never had." He opened a drawer and took out a roll of duct tape. "You like it here, don't you, Carlo? You're going to learn to ride horses and be a cowboy."

Carlo said nothing. He stuck out his lower lip and watched his uncle wrap layer after layer of tape around Patrick's wrists.

Patrick's mind raced. He had to do whatever he could to stay here with Stacy, Carlo and the others. As soon as Abel got him alone, the man would most likely kill him. With his hands bound, Patrick had less chance of overpowering the older man. Years of ranch work had honed his muscles, and the weapon put the odds well in his favor. "Even if Stacy signs papers giving you control of the trust, you won't have legal custody of Carlo," he said.

"What, are you a lawyer, too?" Abel tore the last strip of tape, patted it into place and stepped back. "We've taken care of it."

"Stacy is going to sign over custody of Carlo to us," Willa said.

"I most certainly am not," Stacy said.

"You will unless you want to see the boy hurt." Willa smiled—a horrible grin, made more so by the unnaturally white false teeth that gleamed between her withered lips.

"Mommy, don't let them hurt me." Carlo clung tightly to Stacy, his arms around her neck.

"I won't let them hurt you." If looks really could kill, Willa would have been struck dead right then.

The old woman looked around. "Where's Justine?" she asked.

No one answered.

"Where is Justine?" Willa demanded again.

"What did you do with the nanny?" Abel asked.

"She's fine," Patrick said. "She's in the bathroom upstairs, tied up."

"Well, go untie her, Abel," Willa said.

"I'm a little busy right now, Mother."

"Oh, just shoot him and be done with it. But outside. You don't want to make a mess in here."

Patrick couldn't decide if Mother Giardino was off her rocker or playing the part to unnerve them. He suspected the latter. The old lady looked frail, but her eyes—as well as her tongue—were sharp.

Abel pressed the gun into Patrick's lower back. The hard metal barrel drove into one kidney, reminding him of the damage a bullet at this range would do. The older man grasped the doorknob and turned. Nothing happened. "It's locked," Patrick said.

Abel rewarded this answer with a harder jab of the gun. He unlocked the door and opened it.

"No!" Stacy, still holding Carlo, rushed toward them.

Patrick whirled around in time to see Abel, gun in hand, turn to face her. Her eyes widened in horror and the boy began to wail. "Stacy, hit the floor!" Patrick shouted.

She dropped, throwing her body over Carlo's at the

same time Patrick aimed a mighty kick at Abel's back. The old man went sprawling, the gun flying from his hand. A shot rang out, the bullet splintering the frame of the doorway that led into the hall as it sank into the wood. Stacy screamed, Carlo wailed and Willa shouted curses.

Patrick stepped over the old man on his way to retrieve the gun. Abel grabbed at his ankles and Willa headed toward him with surprising speed despite her walker. Stacy clambered to her feet and pulled Carlo up after her. "The gun!" Patrick called to her. "Get the gun."

She looked around, but apparently didn't see the gun. Patrick raced across the room, thinking he could kick the weapon toward her, but Willa intercepted him, banging him hard in the shins with her walker. Patrick leaned over to shove her aside, but a hard blow to his back knocked him off balance. He turned and Abel landed a solid punch to his chin. Patrick staggered back, trying to maintain his balance.

He heard Stacy coming before he saw her. "Nooo!" she bellowed, and ran at them. She jumped on Abel's back, hands flailing, clawing at his eyes and nose. The old man turned in circles like a rodeo bull trying to throw off a rider. Carlo, still wrapped in the blanket, huddled against the wall and watched the spectacle wide-eyed, his thumb in his mouth.

"Carlo, run!" Stacy shouted. "Run and hide."

The boy hesitated, then turned and raced out the open back door, the blanket trailing behind him like a cape.

Stacy drove her thumb into Abel's eye. With a howl

of rage, the old man grabbed her arm and slung her to the floor, where he began kicking her, his cowboy boots connecting with her ribs with a sickening thud.

Patrick shouted and rushed the old man. Hands still bound behind his back, he had little defense against Abel's fists, but at least the rancher had left Stacy alone. She crawled to the side of the room and leaned against the wall, clutching her side and moaning.

"Stop this! Stop this at once!" Willa shouted. But no one paid her any attention. Abel's fist connected with Patrick's nose and blood spurted. He blinked, trying hard to clear his head. To think. If Abel got hold of the gun again, Patrick was done for, but with his hands tied and Stacy helpless, the old man had the odds in his favor once more.

Abel rushed at him again. Patrick dodged the punch, but the old man still landed a glancing blow. Patrick staggered back.

"Don't let him get out the door!" Willa shouted.

Out of the corner of his eye, Patrick saw Stacy move. She was sliding sideways along the wall, still hunched over and nursing her ribs, or pretending to do so. But she was moving, ever so slowly, toward the handgun that lay in the doorway to the darkened dining room.

"Maybe we should take this outside," Patrick said loudly. "Untie my hands and fight like a man."

"As if insults from a fed mean anything to me." Abel hit him again, a hard blow that snapped his head to one side and sent him staggering again.

"Quit playing with him, Abel," Willa said. "Where is that gun?" She looked around and spotted Stacy. "What do you think you're doing?"

Stacy froze. "I think my ribs are broken." She looked around, as if only just now becoming aware of her surroundings. "Where's Carlo? What have you done with my son?"

"Abel, where is the boy?" Willa asked.

"We'll find him later," Abel said. "When I'm done with the fed here."

"Abel, we should find him now," Willa said.

"He's three years old. He can't drive and he can't walk far in this snow. We'll find him."

"If we lose that boy, we're done for," Willa wailed. "You know that, Abel."

Abel shook his head, looking more annoyed than ever. Patrick leaned back against the counter, stealthily stretching his fingers in search of a knife, a bottle, a frying pan—anything he could use as a weapon.

A heavy footfall on the back steps made them all freeze and look toward the still-open door. A dark figure filled the space, then moved into the room, followed by two burly men with guns drawn.

"What's going on here?" Senator Gary Nordley took in the two battered men, the young woman on the floor and the old one by her walker.

"We caught them trying to steal the boy away." Abel stood up straighter and wiped a smear of blood from his cheek.

"Where is the boy now?" Nordley asked.

"He ran out the door and is hiding somewhere." Abel motioned toward the landscape behind the senator and his bodyguards. "We'll find him. He can't have gone far."

Nordley shook his head. "Abel, you told me you could handle this. Was I wrong to put my faith in you?"

Abel walked over to the dining room and retrieved his gun. "I'm handling it. You don't have to worry."

Nordley scowled at Patrick. Behind him, the two guards focused their weapons on the marshal. "You must be Thompson. I heard you'd been giving my men trouble."

"Hello, Senator. My colleagues told me they suspected you were behind all of this. I had a hard time believing it at first."

"Why wouldn't you believe it? You don't think I'm capable of orchestrating a project like this?"

"A kidnapping is not a project," Stacy snapped. "Murdering people is not a project, you scum."

Nordley turned to her, his expression affable. "Mrs. Giardino. That's not any way to talk to someone to whom your family owes so much."

Stacy struggled to her feet, using the wall for support. Her face was pale, and she was clearly in pain, but her eyes never lost their expression of defiance. "I don't owe you anything."

"If not for me, Sam Giardino would have rotted in prison for the rest of his life."

"I wouldn't have been sorry to see it," Stacy said.

"Maybe not. But this way was so much better. He had a chance to settle his affairs before he died. To make a will giving everything to his only grandson, to be held in trust until the boy is old enough to appreciate the money. In the meantime, there are those of us who can advise him on how to put the funds to the best use."

"That's what this is all about, isn't it?" Patrick said. "You want control of the Giardino family fortune."

"Not for my own selfish aims," Nordley said. "For the good of this country."

"Right. You're a true patriot." Stacy didn't keep the scorn from her voice.

Nordley looked offended. "It takes millions of dollars to run a successful political campaign. In the past I've been obligated to corporate donors and special interests for their contributions. With the Giardino money, I'll be beholden to no one. I'll have the ultimate freedom and the political power to do what's right, without concern for the special interests. And the beautiful irony is that I'll be using corrupt mob money to do good for the American people. I hope Sam Giardino is spinning in his grave at the idea."

"You're crazy," Stacy said.

"Genius is often confused with insanity," Nordley said. "The founding fathers were willing to make sacrifices to turn their ideals into reality. I'm willing to do that, too."

"Killing us isn't some noble sacrifice," Stacy said. "It's murder."

"Who said anything about killing you? You're still useful to me." He turned back to Patrick. "But I have little use for a federal marshal who interfered with things that are none of his business."

"You don't think blood on your hands would look bad to the voters?" Patrick asked.

"There won't be any blood on my hands. If anything, you'll be a hero. An officer who died in the line of duty."

"What are you going to do?" Stacy asked.

The senator ignored her. "Abel, you and Stevie take Marshal Thompson out to one of the barns and take care of things." He motioned toward the door.

"Not the barn," Abel said. "It would upset the horses."

Nordley glowered.

"They're sensitive animals," Abel said.

"Take him to Timbuktu for all I care," Nordley growled. "I don't want to see him again."

"Don't you talk to my son that way," Willa snapped.

Nordley nodded to the old woman. "No disrespect intended."

"You can't kill him!" Stacy protested.

"I told you. I won't be killing anyone," Nordley said.

"You can't let anyone else kill him, either," she said.

"Why not?" Nordley arched one eyebrow, all skepticism.

"You brought me here to sign over control of Carlo's trust. But I already signed it over to Patrick—to Marshal Thompson."

The lines around Nordley's eyes deepened. "Why would you do that?"

"It's because I was going into witness protection," she said. "With a new identity, I couldn't control the trust, so I signed over control to Marshal Thompson. He'll handle things and see that Carlo and I have everything we need."

Patrick couldn't believe what he was hearing. It was a crazy idea, but she was doing a good job of selling it. Nordley turned to him. "Is this true?"

"Yes," he lied.

"What happens if you die?" Abel asked.

"Another agent will take over control of the trust on Carlo's behalf." Was that the right answer?

"You'll spend years in court trying to untangle this," Stacy said. "By the time you're done, Carlo will be grown and you'll be too old to run for president."

"I think you're lying," Nordley said.

"Do you want to take that chance?"

Nordley stuck out his lower lip, considering. "Stevie, you and Ray take these two out to the barn and lock them up," he said after a moment. "Then help the rest of us search for the boy. I'll put in a call to my legal team and get to the bottom of this."

One of the big bruisers grabbed Patrick roughly by the arm and dragged him toward the door. The other man followed with Stacy. Patrick looked into her eyes, intending to offer some reassurance. Instead, she was the one who buoyed his spirits, her eyes shining with triumph over the way she'd tricked the senator.

He wanted to tell her not to get overconfident. Their good luck couldn't last, and when Nordley figured out he'd been had he was liable to take his anger out on them. But no need to add to her worries now. Let her savor her little victory—she'd had few enough things to celebrate lately, and a little respite from worry would help her prepare for the danger ahead.

Chapter Fifteen

Though Stacy's every instinct was to struggle against the man who dragged her toward the barn, she forced herself to relax. Her side ached where Abel had kicked her; if he had broken one of her ribs, struggling would only make things worse. And Patrick wasn't fighting his captor. He had experience in these situations, didn't he? She should follow his lead.

The icy night air hit her like a slap across the face. A shiver convulsed her body and she clenched her teeth to keep them from chattering. As the two thugs led them across the snow she scanned the darkness for some sign of Carlo. He shouldn't be out in this cold. She prayed he'd find a warm place to hide and stay hidden. She didn't want any of these people laying so much as a finger on him ever again.

The barn was dimly lit, smelling of sweet hay and warm horse. One of the animals nickered from the horse boxes that lined both sides of a central passageway. Low-voltage lighting glowed along the floor in front of the boxes, but one of the thugs—Stevie, the senator had called him—flicked a switch and overhead fluorescent lighting flooded the space with a harsh white glow. Several of the horses stirred, their feet shifting on the concrete floor.

"Where should we put them?" the other thug, Ray, asked.

"Over there." Stevie jutted his chin toward a horse box whose door stood open. Half a bale of hay spilled onto the floor inside the box. Stevie led Patrick to an iron ring fastened to one wall in the box and pulled at it. "This should work." He spun Patrick around and wrapped a plastic zip tie around his already-bound wrists and cinched it tight. He wound a thick rope over this, then fastened the rope to the iron ring.

Ray fastened Stacy's wrists together behind her back with a plastic zip tie, then bound her ankles. "Sit on the hay," he told her. "You'll be more comfortable."

She doubted it, but did as he suggested. "Should I tie her to the wall, too?" he asked Stevie.

Stevie was fitting a zip tie around Patrick's ankles. "She won't go anywhere trussed up like a chicken," he said. He pulled the tie tight, then stood.

"Should we gag them?" Ray asked.

"Who's going to hear us if we yell?" Stacy asked.

Stevie looked around, as if searching for a gag, then shook his head. "Forget the gag. We need to go find the kid."

They left the stall, closing the door behind them. She strained her ears, listening as their steps receded. The overhead lights went out, then the barn door opened, creaking on its hinges. As the door closed again a horse across the aisle kicked at its stall, then whinnied.

Stacy looked at Patrick. His lip and one eye were swollen, and dried blood streaked one cheek. He had to be in pain, but the eyes that met hers were calm. Thoughtful. He wasn't panicking, so neither would she. "Now what?" she asked.

"Now we get out of these restraints, find Carlo and get out of Dodge," he said.

"Right. Piece of cake." She struggled against the plastic ties binding her wrists. "But how?"

He looked down at his bound ankles. "These are just plastic zip ties. They probably came out of Abel's garage. I can tell you how to get out of them, then you can free me. How are your ribs?"

She shifted on the hay bale gingerly. "A little sore, but I don't think they're broken, just bruised." Looking at his battered face where Abel had beat him, she felt like a wimp to complain. "Just tell me what I need to do and I'll do it."

"It'll be easier if you slide down until you're sitting on the floor."

She lowered herself to the floor. The concrete was cold, the chill quickly seeping into her. "Now what?"

"Now you've got to bring your arms under your body and around until they're in the front. It'll be easier for you because you're short. How flexible are you?"

"Pretty flexible. I do yoga."

"Then no problem. Take it slowly."

But moving slowly only made her ribs hurt worse, so she forced herself to push past the pain. Leaning back, she worked her wrists under her bottom, then scooted back, gritting her teeth as she contorted her spine into a C and worked her bound hands down the back of her thighs. Knees to chest, she made herself as small as possible. She kicked off her shoes and forced her arms down, ignored the protests from ribs and arm sockets. She sucked in her breath and slid her arms around her feet.

From there, the rest was easy. She eased her bound hands up until they rested at her waist in front of her.

"Good girl," Patrick said. "Now all you have to do is break the cuffs."

She almost sobbed. "How am I going to do that?"

"You're a lot stronger than you think. Raise your hands to about chest height and spread your wrists as far apart as you can. Point your elbows out."

She followed his directions, then looked to him for further instruction.

"Now thrust down with as much force as you can, pulling your arms apart as you do so. Deep breath in.... Now!"

She jerked her arms down, putting everything she had into it, and the plastic snapped apart. She gasped, then stifled a shout of triumph. If any of their captors was close enough to the barn to hear, she didn't want to give herself away. "It worked!"

"Now see if you can untie me. If not, we'll have to find something to use to cut me loose."

Her ankles still bound, she used the wall to push herself to her feet, then hopped awkwardly to him. "I can do this," she said as she fumbled with the rope. "They didn't tie it very well."

"They probably figured with the restraints it was overkill." He turned sideways to give her more room to work. She bit her lip, concentrating on threading the strands of the coarse rope back through the loops of the knot. "There," she said as she pulled the last of the knot loose. "The rope's gone, but what about the rest?"

"Now take off one of your earrings."

"My earring?" She put a hand to the thin gold hoops.

"Just one. And I can't promise this won't break it."

"It's just an earring." She unhooked the bauble and held it out to him.

"Take it and thread the end of the hook between the plastic strap and the little square lock on the zip tie." He turned his back to her and offered up his bound wrists. "It'll be a tight fit, but you should be able to force it in."

She grasped his hand to hold him steady, then wedged the tip of the earring wire into the lock on the cuffs. "I can't get it to go in without bending."

"Keep working at it. A little at a time."

She took a breath, let it out then tried again. This time she was able to ease the wire in a full inch. "What now?"

"Pull on the plastic. See if it will loosen."

She tugged hard on the plastic strap and it began to slide from the lock until it was loose enough for her to remove it from his hands. "What about the duct tape?" She studied the thick layers of silver tape wrapping his wrists.

"Find an end and rip it."

She picked at the tape with one nail, idly noting that she was overdue for a manicure. She almost laughed to be thinking of such things at a time like this.

"What are you smiling about?"

She looked up and found his eyes on her, the affection and tenderness in his expression sending warmth through her. To think she had resented him when they'd first met—been afraid of him, even. She looked away. "I was just thinking how different this is from the life I've been leading—about how sheltered I've been."

"You've done great. I don't know when I've met anyone braver—man or woman."

His praise made her feel about ten feet tall. She pulled the last of the tape from his wrists. He rubbed them, wincing. "Now the ankle bindings—do yours first."

Now that she knew how to use the earring to bypass the locking mechanism on the zip ties, she made short work of their ankle restraints. She was even able to slip her earring back into her ear when she was done. Patrick was still rubbing his wrists, grimacing. She took one of his hands between hers and smoothed the angry red flesh, still sticky with tape residue. "Does it hurt much?"

"I'll live."

She kissed his wrist, his pulse fluttering against her lips. He slid his hands up to cup her cheek and raised her mouth to his. Closing her eyes, she gave herself up to the kiss, all thoughts of danger and lost children and uncertain futures deliberately shoved aside for this one moment of sweetness.

A moment that ended too soon. Patrick pulled away, though he still cradled her face between his hands. "Whatever happens, I want you to know you're the most amazing woman I've ever met," he said.

"Only because I'm with you." She rested her hands on his chest, palms flat over his heart. "You make me believe I can do anything." No one—not her parents or old boyfriends or her husband—had ever had that kind of confidence in her. She could have loved him for that alone.

"That's because you can." He kissed her forehead, then turned toward the door. "Come on. We have to find Carlo before they do." He grasped the doorknob. It turned easily enough, but the door refused to budge. He shoved against it, but the heavy wooden door scarcely moved.

"What is it?" Stacy tried to see around him. "What's wrong?"

He turned back to her, his face grim. "There's a bolt thrown over the door from the outside. We can't get out."

CARLO WAS COLD. The night air cut through his thin pajamas and his socks were soaked from running through the snow. The snow was cold on his hands, but when he walked now, the snow burned his feet. How could the snow be both hot and cold?

He huddled between the water barrels on the side of the house and looked out at the darkness. He was afraid of the dark. Even in the daytime, he had never been far from the house alone. Uncle Abel said there were wild animals out there—coyotes and bears that would eat little boys.

He could hear people calling his name—Uncle Abel and other men he didn't know. He didn't answer them, and tried to make himself smaller in the narrow space between the two water barrels. He'd decided to hide here because he could see the lights of the yard from here. He could see the barn and the cars and other familiar things.

He was so cold. His teeth chattered and his whole body shook. Even with his knees drawn up to his chin and his arms wrapped around his legs, he was still cold. He had lost the blanket somewhere while he was running; he couldn't remember where. When he breathed out, his breath made little clouds in front of his face.

The voices had moved around to behind the house now. Would they come around here eventually? What would Uncle Abel and the men do if they found him? Uncle Abel was usually nice, but tonight he had looked angry. He'd been very angry at Mommy and the man with her. Carlo didn't like it when people were angry.

His daddy had been angry a lot, and had yelled at Mommy. Sometimes he'd made her cry, and that made Carlo sad and mad and afraid, all at the same time.

Where was Mommy now? She hadn't been here for so long, then tonight she had finally come, and then she'd told him to run away. None of it made sense.

He put his head on his knees and closed his eyes. Maybe if he went to sleep he'd dream about being some place warm.

The barn was warm. The horses made it warm. The horses were big, and they scared him a little, but he liked to watch them from a distance. The other day Uncle Abel had put him up in the saddle in front of him and walked the horse around the corral. Carlo had never been so high up before. He loved the feel of the horse rocking beneath him. Uncle Abel had promised to teach him to ride when he was bigger. Carlo would have his own pony and learn to be a cowboy.

He could go to the barn and hide. He'd be warm and if he couldn't sleep, he could watch the horses.

He stood and peered around the barrels. The yard was quiet and empty. He dashed across the wide strip of blackness between the house and the barn. When he reached the deeper shadows beside the barn, he was out of breath and his side hurt from running. His feet still burned, but the rest of him felt a little warmer.

He felt his way around the side of the building to the door to the feed room. Standing on tiptoe, he could just reach the doorknob. He opened it and went inside. The door from the feed room to the main barn stood open. Low-voltage lights illuminated the central walkway between the horse boxes. The barn cat, Matilda, came up and leaned against his legs. He ran his hand along the soft fur of her back and smiled. "Good kitty," he whispered. He didn't want to wake the horses, who were probably sleeping.

He pulled a saddle blanket from a pile by the door and lay down on a bale of hay beside the feed bins. The cat curled up against him. He was warmer now, and sleepy. Maybe in the morning, he'd see Mommy again.

Chapter Sixteen

Patrick studied the door on the horse box. It was made of heavy wood with forged iron hinges on the outside. It was built to contain animals weighing hundreds of pounds. But he couldn't accept that there wasn't some way out. "Stand back," he told Stacy.

When she'd moved out of the way, he took a few steps back, rushing the door. He slammed into the heavy wood, the impact reverberating through his already battered body, rattling his teeth and blurring his vision. The door didn't budge.

"I don't believe this!" Stacy wailed. "We've got to get out of here and find Carlo!" Her voice rose in a shout of frustration. Patrick felt like shouting with her. Instead, he looked around the bare stall for anything he could use to hack or pry at the door.

"Mommy? Mommy, where are you?"

He froze and looked to Stacy, whose eyes locked with his. "Carlo?" She ran to the door and stood on tiptoe, as close to the rectangular wooden vent at the top of the door as she could get. "Carlo, Mommy is here, in the horse box."

Shuffling sounds—small feet on concrete and hay— moved toward them. "Mommy, I want to see you."

"I'm in the horse box, baby. Someone locked the door and I can't get out. I need you to help me."

Small fists pounded on the door. "Come out, Mommy."

Stacy knelt now, making herself the height of a three-year-old. "I'll come out, baby. But I need your help. Look up, at the top of the door. Do you see the bolt?"

"Uh-huh."

"Can you climb on something and get to that bolt? Is there a feed bucket or something you can stand on?"

"There's a bucket in the feed room."

"Then be a good boy and get it and bring it over to the door."

He didn't answer, but Patrick thought he must have moved away. Stacy closed her eyes and pressed her forehead against the door. Patrick moved to put a hand to her shoulder. She must be exhausted, but they'd all be out of here soon, she and Carlo safe.

Something scraped on the concrete. "I got the bucket!" Carlo shouted.

"Good. Now turn it upside down and put it in front of the door. Climb on top of it, but be careful."

"Don't worry, Mommy. I'm a good climber."

"I'm sure you are. But be careful."

Patrick scarcely dared to breathe while they waited. The last thing they needed was the boy falling and busting his head on the concrete floor. The bucket rattled and the boy beat his fists against the door. "I made it!"

"Great," Stacy said. "Now reach up and pull back the bolt."

"I have to stand on tippy-toes." Scrabbling noises, accompanied by little grunts. "It's in there really hard."

"You're a strong boy. Pull hard."

A metallic *thunk* announced the bolt's moving. "I did it!" Carlo crowed. "I opened the door."

"That's wonderful, baby. Now climb down and move away from the door so I can come out."

More scraping and fumbling with the bucket. "You can come out now, Mommy."

Stacy eased open the door. Carlo hurtled into her arms. "What were you doing in there, Mommy?" he asked, his arms around her neck. "Were you hiding?"

"That's right, baby." She stroked his hair and kissed his cheek. "We were hiding, but not from you."

The boy looked over her shoulder at Patrick, eyes wide. "I was hiding," he said. "But I got cold, so I came into the barn."

"You did great." She hefted the boy onto her hip and turned to Patrick. "Can we go now?"

"In a minute." He scanned the passageway and the area around the stalls, then slipped into the feed room, looking for anything he could use as a weapon. He found a short-bladed knife on a shelf there and pocketed it. He picked up a horse blanket and took it to Stacy. "Wrap the boy up in this."

She tucked the blanket around her son. "When we get to the car, you'll be a lot warmer," she said.

One hand resting lightly on Stacy's shoulder, Patrick leaned in to address the little boy in her arms. "We're going to sneak past your uncle and his guards and go to my car, which is parked on the road through the woods. It's kind of a long way for your mom to carry a big guy like you. Would you let me carry you?"

Carlo put his thumb in his mouth and looked at his

mother. "It's all right," she said. "I'll be right here be-side you."

The boy nodded, then held his arms out to Patrick. That simple gesture of trust brought a lump to his throat. He settled the boy against his chest; the weight felt good there. Right. Stacy's eyes met his across the top of the boy's head and she offered a weary smile. "Thanks," she whispered.

He should be thanking her. Until he'd met her, his life had revolved around work and duty. He still took those things seriously, but she made him see beyond the job, to other things that might matter to him. "Let's go," he said. "Stay close to me and keep to the shadows."

Once he'd determined the coast was clear, they left the barn. The yard was silent and still, not so much as a moth fluttering around the light over the back steps of the house. No one called Carlo's name or ran through the yard. Had they called off the search for now, or taken it farther afield?

He guided Stacy around the perimeter of the light, the knife clutched in one hand, ready to lash out at any-one who came near. Once they reached the pasture and the deeper darkness there, they'd retrieve their snow-shoes and be able to move faster. They wouldn't stop again until they reached the car. In half an hour they'd be headed toward Denver, where he'd find a safe house for Stacy and her son until the task force had rounded up Nordley and Uncle Abel and everyone else involved.

They'd reached the edge of the yard when a woman's scream tore apart the night silence. He whirled and saw a woman racing across the yard, a man chasing after her. The man grabbed the woman by her long hair and dragged her back toward the house. "The babysitter," Stacy whispered.

"Why is he hurting Justine?" Carlo asked.

"I don't know, baby." Stacy rubbed his back and looked at Patrick with eyes full of questions.

"That was one of Nordley's thugs," Patrick said. "Maybe she panicked and threatened to go to the authorities."

"Maybe so." She continued rubbing Carlo's back. "Was Justine nice to you, honey?"

"She was real nice. So were Uncle Abel and Grandma." His lower lip trembled. "When will I see them again? Uncle Abel promised me a pony."

Before she could answer, the back door to the house flew open once more. This time a man rushed down the steps, followed by one of the thugs. "Is that Uncle Abel?" Stacy asked.

The first man was Abel. He and the younger, burlier man struggled, then three gunshots sounded, *Pop! Pop! Pop!* like firecrackers in the winter stillness. Abel slumped to the ground, and a dark stain formed on the snow. Patrick cradled Carlo's head against his shoulder, turned away so the boy wouldn't see.

"What's happening?" Stacy whispered, as she pulled the blanket over Carlo's head.

"Mo-om! What are you doing?" He tried to push the blanket away, but she held it in place.

"You don't have a hat. I don't want your head to get cold," she said.

The younger man dragged Abel back into the house. Patrick couldn't tell if the old man was alive or dead.

"Do you think Nordley turned on him?" Stacy asked. "We have to do something."

"You really want to help these people?"

"They were kind to Carlo. And they're the only relatives he has left. If the senator is attacking them…"

She was right. He couldn't abandon two old people and the babysitter to Nordley's thugs. "Let me get you and Carlo to the car, then I'll come back."

"No. I won't leave you. And two people against Nordley are better than one."

Not when one of the people was a woman with a little boy to look after, but he didn't bother to say it. He knew Stacy well enough by now to know he wouldn't be able to convince her to leave. "We need a way to draw them out," he said. "If we try to charge the house, they have the advantage."

"Let's find a safe place to leave Carlo." She looked around the compound. "I wish we had someplace warmer."

"That's it." Patrick felt the surge of excitement that accompanied a good idea, one he knew would succeed. "We need to start a fire. That will draw them out of the house, plus alert the agents who are watching the place."

"How are we going to start a fire?" she asked. "We don't have any matches."

"Leave that to me."

The building farthest from the house in the ranch compound was an open-sided shed half filled with hay. If Patrick could get the hay going, it would make a bright, hot fire with a lot of smoke, perfect for raising the alarm. He searched the feed room and grabbed a flashlight. Further searching among the supplies on the shelves produced a wad of steel wool. "What are you going to do with that?" Stacy asked.

"I'm going to start a fire. Come on. Let's get to the hay barn."

Two minutes later they crouched in the deep shadow of the barn. Patrick pulled hay loose from the bales until he had a foot-high pile in the open area at one end of the shed. Then he unscrewed the top from the flashlight and set the two batteries next to each other nestled in the hay. He tore off a piece of steel wool. "Take Carlo to the end of the shed," he told Stacy. "Just to be safe."

She did as he asked. He dropped the steel wool on top of the batteries, bridging the gap between the posts. The batteries sparked and the wool burst into flames. He nudged the burning wool onto the hay, which caught quickly. Within seconds a line of fire crept across the floor, toward the bulk of the hay stacked at the end of the shed.

Patrick joined Stacy and Carlo just outside the building. "Now we wait." He started toward the house. When Nordley or his thugs emerged, Patrick would be ready.

BY THE TIME they reached the house, flames had climbed to the roof of the hay shed. The fire crackled and popped like small-arms fire and smoke filled the air, stinging the nose. The agents watching the ranch would have seen the blaze by now, and the people in the house were bound to notice soon. Gaze fixed on the back door, Patrick saw the first movement and pulled Stacy and the boy into the deeper shadows beside the house as the door burst open and Senator Nordley, followed by

Stevie, ran out. "Get the hose," Nordley shouted. "I'll turn on the water!"

"Abel must be hurt badly," Stacy whispered, "if he's not coming to help."

Patrick nodded and started toward the steps, but Stacy rushed past him, Carlo in her arms. He grabbed her wrist and pulled her back. "Let me go in first," he said.

She nodded. "Of course." She stepped back to let him pass. "I'm just worried about Abel and Willa."

Right. The people who had kidnapped her child and threatened to kill her. But they'd been kind to the boy, and something about them had touched her. Despite her tough attitude, Stacy had a tender heart. Ordinary things—not littering and taking care of family— mattered to her. "Here's the plan," he said. "I go in first. We know there's just one guard. I'll overpower him. Don't come in until I give you the signal."

She frowned. "But—"

"You need to stay here with Carlo."

She nodded. "All right." She moved to the side of the door with the boy, into the shadows on the far side of the steps. Knife at the ready, Patrick opened the door and slipped inside.

The kitchen was deserted, though the sound of the television still drifted from the living room. He peered into the room and saw the two women seated side by side on the sofa. The coffee table had been shoved out of the way and Abel lay on the floor at the women's feet, his face pale, eyes closed.

The guard stood a few feet away, cradling an AR-15, his head turned so he could look out the window toward the blazing hay shed. To reach the guard, Patrick would have to approach from the kitchen, making him an easy target.

Someone moaned, low and painful. "He's awake," Willa said, and leaned toward her son.

So Abel wasn't dead, though from here Patrick couldn't tell how badly he was injured. The old man moaned again, louder.

"Don't move," the guard ordered.

But both women had already dropped to their knees and were fussing over the injured man. The guard turned from the window and came over to them, his back to Patrick.

Patrick charged. In three strides he crossed the room and drove the knife blade between the guard's ribs. The man screamed and loosened his grip on the rifle enough for Patrick to wrestle it from him. The man froze when the marshal pointed the gun at his chest. "Facedown on the floor," Patrick ordered.

"I'm bleeding." The guard looked at the blood seeping down his side.

"You'll bleed more if you don't do as I tell you."

The guard lowered himself to the floor and lay on his stomach. Patrick turned his attention to the women. "We need something to tie him up," he said.

The younger woman, Justine, who was near Abel's age, tugged a scarf from around her neck. "You can use this."

"You use it." Patrick motioned with the gun. "Tie his hands, then find something to tie his feet."

She nodded and knelt beside the guard while Patrick

turned his attention to Abel. Willa leaned over her son. "Do something," she pleaded. "You can't let him die."

Abel appeared to have been shot in the right shoulder, and again in the thigh. Blood pooled around him on the floor, but had started to clot. He was pale and his breathing was labored, but when Patrick checked his pulse, it beat steady and strong, if a little rapid. "What happened?" he asked.

"He overheard the senator tell one of his men that when they found Carlo they should just kill him," Willa said. "Then Abel, as next of kin, could petition the court to get the money. Abel couldn't let that happen. Justine ran out, thinking she would find the boy first and hide him. Abel tried to distract the senator. They got into an argument and one of the guards shot him. Then they ordered us all in here." She stroked her son's forehead. "We needed the money to help save the ranch, but we fell in love with Carlo. We couldn't let that man hurt him."

Justine had finished tying up the guard. "Let me get some things to clean his wounds," she said.

"Of course." Patrick stepped back. "If you have a first aid kit, we can bandage him up."

"Where is Carlo?" Justine asked. "Do you know?"

"He and his mother are waiting outside. I'll get them now."

He returned to the kitchen and opened the back door. "Stacy?" he called.

She stepped out of the shadows, Carlo in her arms. Relief filled him; though he'd only left her a short time, there'd been a chance Nordley or Stevie would find her. Knowing she was safe eased some of his tension.

"Come inside." He held the door wider. "Everyone is in the living room. Any sign of Nordley and Stevie?"

"No. They must still be at the hay barn."

He glanced toward the barn. The flames had climbed higher and illuminated the night. They must be visible for miles.

He did a quick check around the outside of house and saw nothing to alarm him, though shouts came from the direction of the hay barn. When he returned to the living room he found Abel sitting up, propped against the sofa. Justine and Willa sat on either side of him. Stacy sat in the chair opposite, Carlo in her lap. The boy stared at his uncle, eyes wide, thumb in his mouth.

"Give me a gun," Abel said when he saw Patrick. "I want to shoot Nordley myself when he comes back."

"I thought you and the senator were friends."

"Sure. A friend who shot me." His mouth twisted in disgust. "We were never friends."

"How did you get involved with him in the first place?" Patrick asked.

"Don't badger him," Willa said. "He's hurt."

"He needs to know what he's dealing with," Abel said. He shifted, as if trying to get comfortable when that was impossible. After a second, he spoke again. "Sam sent him to me. When the economy was good I took out a second mortgage on the ranch to expand the operation. Then things went south. The land wasn't worth what it was, people weren't buying expensive horses, but the stock still had to eat. The bank still wanted to be paid. I asked Sam to help me. I figured criminals were the one bunch that were still doing well no matter what the stock market was up to."

He coughed, and Willa patted his shoulder. "You shouldn't talk so much," she said, and glared at Patrick.

Abel waved her away. "Sam said he couldn't help me, but he said he knew someone who could. Nordley came to see me and said if I'd do him a few favors, he'd pay off the mortgage. All that debt, gone."

"What did he ask you to do?" Stacy asked.

"That was the thing. It was nothing. He sent a couple men to stay here a few days. They rode around, walked the property, didn't bother anybody. He said he wanted to use the place as a retreat. They stayed in the bunkhouse, didn't bother anybody. He bought the mortgage from the bank and said as long as I cooperated, I didn't have anything to worry about. I know now he was just setting me up. Playing me for a fool."

"He couldn't have known Sam would die," Stacy said.

"I think he planned a hit on Sam before the feds got involved and did the dirty work for him," Abel said. "Nordley has that kind of nerve. He thinks he's a genius and everyone else are fools."

"After Sam died, he asked if we would look after Carlo." Willa took up the story. "He told us the mother didn't want the boy and he needed to be with family."

"He lied." Stacy hugged Carlo closer.

Willa ignored her. "Of course we would look after my great-grandson. Two of the senator's men brought him here one night."

"That's when Nordley told me the rest of the plan," Abel said. "That we were supposed to use the boy to get control of the money. I knew about the will. One of the last times I talked to Sam, he bragged about how smart he was, giving the money to the boy and tying it up in a trust. I guess Sam told his buddy Nordley about the will, too, but not about the boy's mother having control of the trust. That's why he ordered his men to just bring the boy here. When I told Nordley the boy's mother had control, he was angry. He said we'd have to get Stacy here and force her to sign over everything." His shoulders sagged. "By then I was in too deep. I couldn't see a way out."

"You'd have let him kill me for money," Stacy said.

"He would have killed me. He would have killed all of us." Abel shook his head. "I never wanted anything to do with the family business. All I wanted was to ranch. Sam said I'd betrayed the family. I figured involving me with Nordley was his way of getting back at me."

"We love the boy." Willa addressed Stacy directly. "We never would have hurt him."

Stacy nodded. "He loves you, too. He said you were good to him." She stood as if to go to the old woman, just as the window next to Patrick's head exploded and a bullet thudded into the wall behind the sofa.

"Everyone down!" Patrick shouted. He crouched beside the window, trying to glimpse the shooter in the darkness. Willa and Justine sobbed and Abel muttered curses and pleaded again for someone to give him a gun. More shots hit the outside of the house around the window. Patrick decided there was just a single shooter, but he was determined to keep them pinned down. Where was the other man—probably Nordley—and what was he up to?

Stacy's scream rose above the other background

noise, accompanied by the sounds of a struggle. "He's got Carlo!"

Patrick whirled and found the senator, his face streaked with soot, hair in wild disarray, clutching the boy to his chest. He pressed the muzzle of a pistol against the child's temple. "Unless you want me to kill the boy now, you'll put down that rifle and let me leave," Nordley rasped.

The shooter outside had silenced his weapon, also. Now came the rev of an engine, very near the house. "I believe that's my ride," Nordley said.

Patrick carefully lowered the rifle to the floor, every muscle protesting as the senator dragged a terrified Carlo toward the door. He looked for a way—any way—to stop the abduction, but the risk was too great. He believed Nordley wouldn't hesitate to pull the trigger.

Nordley made it out the door and down the front steps. Patrick, Stacy and Willa followed, keeping their distance, but unable to look away as the senator walked backward toward the car. He was even with the back bumper when Carlo, who had hung limp in his arms, suddenly came to life. The boy bit down hard on Nordley's arm and flailed his legs, landing a hard kick in Nordley's crotch. Nordley cried out and the gun went off.

Stacy screamed and covered her eyes with her hands. "It's all right," Patrick told her. "Carlo's free." The boy raced toward them. Nordley, doubled over, tried to fire after him, but his aim was wild.

Patrick grabbed up the boy and swept him into the house, herding the women before him. He retrieved the rifle and raced to the door once more, but Nordley was already in the car, driving away. A siren screamed in the distance, approaching fast.

Stacy, Carlo in her arms, came to stand behind him. "Are you all right, buddy?" Patrick asked.

"I didn't want to go with that bad man."

"You did good, darling." Stacy kissed him. "So very good. You were so brave." She watched Nordley's car careen down the driveway. "He's going to get away."

"Maybe not." The sound of screeching tires, crushed metal and breaking glass punctuated this statement. Patrick raced down the drive, running hard, but by the time he reached the crash site at the entrance to the ranch, men swarmed over the wreckage of a government-issue SUV and Nordley's Jeep.

Two men dragged Stevie out of the driver's side. The guard was able to stand on his own, though blood ran from a cut on his head. The passenger side of the vehicle was crushed.

"We think the passenger is Nordley." Special Agent Sullivan, looking sharp in a black ballistics vest over his black suit, came to stand beside Patrick. "We'll know more once we've cut him out and loaded him into the ambulance."

"It's him," Patrick said. "Is he alive?"

"From the sound of it, he is," Sullivan said. "And cussing a blue streak." He glanced down the drive. "What's the situation at the house?"

"An older man, the ranch owner, Abel Giardino, is shot. He needs an ambulance. Three women and the boy are frightened, but okay."

"I'm not going to ask you right now why you're here after I told you to stay away."

Patrick met the other man's eyes, refusing to back down. "I had a job to do, just like you. I had to keep Stacy Giardino and her child safe."

"In doing so, you forced Nordley's hand." He looked back at the car, where emergency personnel were prying apart the passenger door to get to the senator. "He might not have been so careless if not for you."

"You were right—he's behind all of this. He intended to use the boy to gain control of the Giardino money. He blackmailed Abel and Willa into helping him."

"I'll need your full report as soon as possible. And we'll want to interview the Giardinos and anyone else who lives here."

"We can talk about all that later. I have to take care of Stacy and her son now." He turned to walk back to the house.

"You could lose your job over this," Sullivan said. "Or at least get a ding on your record."

Maybe so. But he'd done what he knew was right, and he could live with that. "I guess we'll see."

"Do you think she's worth all this trouble?"

He smiled, though his back was to Sullivan. "Yes," he said. "Yes, she is." He walked faster, back to the house and back to Stacy. The sooner this was over and they were together, the better.

STACY REMAINED IN the house with Carlo while Willa and Justine followed the emergency personnel who carried the stretcher on which Abel lay. The old man was responsive and the EMTs pronounced him stable. "Will Uncle Abel be okay?" Carlo asked.

"He will." She forced a smile for her son's sake. "Tomorrow or the next day, we'll see if we can visit him in the hospital. I know he'd like that."

"Okay." Carlo buried his head against her chest and closed his eyes. He must be exhausted; she was. But too many things remained unsettled for her to rest easily.

As the EMTs and the two older women exited the house, Patrick squeezed past them. He still carried the weapon, though it was slung at his side. Dark blood smeared his shoulder and dark half-moons ringed his eyes. Yet she'd never seen a better sight. "You doing okay?" he asked.

She nodded. "Just tired. And I need to get Carlo to bed."

"I'll find someone to give us a ride to my Jeep and take you back to the hotel."

"I don't have to go to some police station and answer a bunch of questions about what happened?"

"There'll be time enough for that later. Right now you two need your rest."

"What will you do?"

"I'm still in charge of keeping you safe."

"Then you won't leave us." Relief surged through her. She'd been afraid that now that she and Carlo were out of danger, he'd be anxious to be rid of them. Sure, he'd said and done a lot of things over the past few days to make her think he cared for her, but maybe that had all been part of him gaining her confidence. Maybe now that he didn't have to be with her, he'd feel differently. "What will happen now?" she asked—the question she had repeatedly asked him throughout this ordeal. He always had an answer that reassured her and kept her going.

"Senator Nordley will face charges—kidnapping, attempted murder, aiding a felon.... I'm sure there are others. Abel could be charged, too, but I'm betting he can work a plea deal if he agrees to testify against Nordley. Especially if you don't press the issue."

She shook her head. "I believe his story about being caught up in Nordley's schemes. I meant, what will happen to me? Do I have to remain in custody?"

"No. But I'll help you get settled."

"I still don't want to be in WITSEC. There's no reason for that now."

"I wasn't talking about WITSEC."

"You mean I'm on my own?"

"Only if you want to be."

The warmth was gone from his voice, replaced by an anxious tone. He shifted nervously and studied her face, as if trying to decipher her thoughts. The man who was always so confident and sure of himself looked lost. "What's wrong?" she asked. "Why are you acting so weird?"

"Because I don't know how else to act." He touched her shoulder, a tentative brush of two fingers against her collarbone. "Would you think I was crazy if I told you I loved you?"

"That is crazy talk," she said, even as her heart raced.

He ran a hand through his hair so that the blond strands stood on end. "I know we've only known each other a few days. But in that time I feel I've gotten to know you and...I've never felt about anyone the way I feel about you. I think you're amazing—smart and brave and strong, and a great mother, a beautiful, sexy lover.... I just... I can't deal with the idea of losing you."

"You don't have to lose me."

His eyes searched hers again. "What are you saying?"

She shifted Carlo, who had fallen asleep, to her other side. "You live in Denver, right?"

He nodded.

"I could move to Denver," she said. "I can find a job, maybe even go back to school. We could see each other—see how we do together in the real world."

"I'd like that."

She almost laughed. "That's all you can say?"

In answer, he pulled her close and kissed her. Lips locked to hers, he lifted both her and Carlo off the ground. When their lips parted, they were both breathless. "I'd love that, Stacy Giardino," he said. "I love you."

"I love you, too, Patrick Thompson. As crazy as we both are—I love you."

Epilogue

One year later

Stacy looked out the window of the courthouse at the crowd of reporters waiting at the bottom of the steps. News vans lined the street and the microphones and cameras were three deep. "I can't believe they all want to talk to me," she said.

Patrick, looking more handsome than ever in a suit and tie, put a reassuring hand to her back. "Your testimony was crucial in convicting Senator Nordley, not to mention the human-interest angle of an ordinary woman being caught up in a mob family, then having to fight to save her child—the public loves you."

"I'll be happy when things settle down and I'm no longer in the spotlight." She straightened the jacket of her chic suit. The bold purple-and-black colors made her stand out in the sea of lawyerly gray. "Guess we'd better get this over with."

The door to the anteroom where she and Patrick had retreated opened and Carlo raced in. "Mama, we're going to be on TV!" he said.

"Looks like it." She knelt to smooth his tie. "You

remember what I told you? Mind your manners and don't speak unless someone asks you a question."

He nodded. "Aunt Deborah already told me all that."

Stacy looked up at the woman who had followed Carlo into the room. Deborah Thompson had the same blond hair and blue eyes as her brother, but she was petite and delicate. She smiled at Stacy. "Are you ready?"

Stacy stood and took a deep breath. "I think so."

Deborah came and slipped her arm around Stacy's shoulder. "You're going to do great. Just remember all we talked about."

Stacy nodded. For almost a year now she'd been seeing Deborah once a week for counseling sessions. It turned out Patrick's sister was a psychologist. A former battered wife herself, she specialized in helping other women who'd been in abusive situations.

With brother and sister on either side of her and Carlo running ahead, Stacy made her way out to the reporters. Camera flashes flared and voices shouted questions. She read the statement she'd prepared, thanking federal agents and prosecutors for bringing a serious predator and criminal to justice.

"What are your plans now that the trial is over?" a reporter asked.

"I've been accepted into University of Denver law school," she said. "I'll start classes there in a few weeks."

"Are the rumors about you and Marshal Thompson true?" another voice shouted.

"Is that an engagement ring you're wearing?" asked someone else.

Stacy smiled down at the diamond solitaire on the

third finger of her left hand. Patrick had given it to her at dinner last night, when they'd known for sure the trial would end today. His proposal hadn't been a surprise; they'd been inseparable for the past year. So her answer hadn't been unexpected, either.

"Stacy has done me the honor of agreeing to be my wife." Patrick had stepped up to the mic beside her.

"What do you think of that, Carlo?" someone asked.

Patrick lifted the little boy to the microphone so he could answer. "I think he'll be a good dad," Carlo said. When some in the crowd laughed, he buried his face in Patrick's shoulder, suddenly shy.

"That's all the time we have for questions." The chief prosecutor stepped in to guide them away from the microphones. They retreated back into the courthouse. Patrick's car was parked in the underground garage, making a discreet getaway easier.

"You did great." Deborah patted her shoulder. "I'll see you two later." She kissed Stacy's cheek, then repeated the gesture with Patrick and Carlo.

"How do you feel?" Patrick asked Stacy, after he'd set Carlo down. The little boy ran ahead to the elevator. "Are you relieved it's all over?"

"I'm relieved the trial is behind us. As for the rest..." She smiled and took his arm. "I feel like my life is finally beginning. I have school to look forward to, and the wedding, and us being together as a family. A real family, full of love and support. That's a first for me."

"Me, too." He stopped walking and turned toward her. "Have I told you lately how much I love you?"

"Not in the past half hour."

He kissed her lightly. "It's true." Then he deepened the kiss, pulling her close.

"You're embarrassing me!" Carlo's voice rang through the lobby.

"Better get used to it," Patrick called. "Your mother and I plan to spend the rest of our lives embarrassing you."

Stacy rested her forehead against Patrick's shoulder, laughing. A year ago, she wouldn't have believed she could be so happy. One man—and love—had made all the difference.

* * * * *

#1485 JOSH

The Lawmen of Silver Creek Ranch
by Delores Fossen

After a near-fatal attack, FBI agent Josh Ryland returns to his Texas hometown to recuperate. There, he encounters an old flame who's not only pregnant with his child, but in grave danger.

#1486 THE LEGEND OF SMUGGLER'S CAVE

Bitterwood P.D. • by Paula Graves

Dalton Hale is determined to protect Briar Blackwood from her husband's killer. Can he find the murderer without losing his heart?

#1487 THE BRIDGE

Brody Law • by Carol Ericson

Elise Duran escaped The Alphabet Killer once, but SFPD detective Sean Brody is the only one who can stop the killer from getting to "the one that got away."

#1488 RELENTLESS

Corcoran Team • by HelenKay Dimon

A first date turns into a fight for survival when NCIS agent Ben Tanner has to keep Jocelyn Raine out of the hands of men intent on revenge.

#1489 PRIMAL INSTINCT

by Janie Crouch

FBI agent Connor Perigo turns to profiler Adrienne Jeffries for help catching a killer, but can Connor capture him before Adrienne becomes a victim?

#1490 DIAGNOSIS: ATTRACTION

Mindbenders • by Rebecca York

When a car accident takes away Elizabeth Forester's memories, only Dr. Matthew Delano's touch can restore her past and protect her future.

YOU CAN FIND MORE INFORMATION ON UPCOMING HARLEQUIN® TITLES, FREE EXCERPTS AND MORE AT WWW.HARLEQUIN.COM.

HICNM0314

REQUEST YOUR FREE BOOKS!
2 FREE NOVELS PLUS 2 FREE GIFTS!

HARLEQUIN
INTRIGUE
BREATHTAKING ROMANTIC SUSPENSE

*A single mom puts her life, and the life of her little boy,
in the hands of a sexy, protective county prosecutor…*

It was well after nine when Dalton finally called Briar to
tell her he was coming up the front walkway. She hurried to
unlock the door and let him in. "All stitched up?"

He nodded. "Want to see my wound?"

Smiling, she shook her head. "You hungry? Logan and
I had chicken soup for dinner. I can heat some up for you."

He caught her hand as she moved toward the kitchen, his
fingers warm and firm around hers. "Doyle and I grabbed a
burger on the way home."

"How'd that go?" She waited for him to let go of her
hand, but he twined his fingers with hers instead, leading
her over to the sofa. He sat heavily, tugging her down beside him.

"It went…better than I expected. He wasn't a complete
smart-ass, and I tried not to be a defensive jerk. So…prog-
ress." He gave her hands a light squeeze. "Logan asleep?"

She looked down at their twined hands, her gaze drawn
by the intersection of her fair skin and his tanned fingers.
"About thirty minutes ago. We had to read a couple of extra
stories, and he was worried that you weren't home yet, but
I explained you had to go somewhere with your brother. I
also promised you'd look in on him before you go to bed.
You don't have to, though. Once he falls asleep, it takes a
bulldozer to wake him. He wouldn't know you were there."

"I'll know," he said, rolling his head toward her.

She met his gaze, a ripple of pure feminine awareness rolling through her, setting off a dozen tingles along her spine.

But was she woman enough to deal with a man like Dalton? A man who'd lived a life of privilege she couldn't even begin to imagine, much less understand? A man with his own demons that made her day-to-day struggles seem like bumps in the road in comparison?

"Last night," he murmured, "I wanted to kiss you."

She closed her eyes, overwhelmed by his raw honesty. "I know."

"I still do."

Can Briar and Dalton escape the clutches of an elusive enemy and have the happy future they both crave? Find out in THE LEGEND OF SMUGGLER'S CAVE by award-winning author Paula Graves, available April 2014 wherever Harlequin® Intrigue® books and ebooks are sold.

HARLEQUIN®

INTRIGUE®

USA TODAY BESTSELLING AUTHOR
DELORES FOSSEN RETURNS TO
SILVER CREEK WITH THE SCORCHING
STORY OF A TEXAS LAWMAN WHO'LL
RISK EVERYTHING TO SAVE HIS
EX-LOVE—AND HIS UNBORN CHILD...

FBI agent turned Texas deputy Josh Ryland is stunned to find pregnant hostages on a routine check for suspicious activity at a remote ranch. Even more shocking is the identity of one of the captives. Five months ago, Josh and FBI special agent Jaycee Finney shared a weekend of passion that ended badly. Now she's in danger—and claims he's her baby's father.

Jaycee owes Josh the truth. After her unwitting reckless behavior almost got him killed, the cowboy cop has good reason not to trust her. But with the ruthless mastermind of a black market baby ring gunning for her, it's Jaycee who has to trust Josh with her life...and the life of their child.

JOSH
BY DELORES FOSSEN

Available April 2014, only from Harlequin® Intrigue®.

HI69752